ESTHER

A
Jerusalem
Love Story

Dvora Waysman

SiMCHA
PRESS
An Imprint of Health Communications, Inc.®

Deerfield Beach, Florida
www.simchapress.com

Library of Congress Cataloging-in-Publication Data

Waysman, Dvora.
    Esther : a Jerusalem love story / Dvora Waysman.
      p.   cm.
    ISBN 1-55874-822-9 (alk. paper)
    1. Women novelists—Fiction.   2. Journalists—Fiction.
  3. Australians—Jerusalem—Fiction.   4. Jews—Jerusalem—
Fiction.   5. Jerusalem—Fiction.   I. Title.

PR9510.9.W39 E8 2000
823'.914—dc21

                                         00-058841

©2000 Dvora Waysman
ISBN 1-55874-822-9

Simcha Press, its Logos and Marks are trademarks of Health Communications, Inc.

Publisher: Simcha Press
              An Imprint of Health Communications, Inc.
              3201 S.W. 15th Street
              Deerfield Beach, FL 33442-8190

Cover design by Larissa Hise
Inside book design by Dawn Grove

This novel is dedicated
to two important Esthers in my life:

In memory of Esther Patterson, R.A.,
a brilliant artist and source of wisdom and love.

For my daughter-in-law,
Esther Waysman, who is also my friend.

. . . when I keep
Calmly the count of my own life and see
On what poor stuff my manhood's dreams
were fed
Till I, too, learned what dole of vanity
Will serve a human soul for bread
—Then I remember that I once was young
And lived with Esther the world's gods among.

—Wilfred Scawen Blunt, 1840–1922

Acknowledgments

My warm thanks go to Rita Rosenkranz, my agent; Gail Kinn, a sensitive and talented editor; and Kim Weiss of HCI, who believed in me and encouraged me from the beginning. Also thanks to some voices from the past: editor Dan Leon and photographer Douglas Guthrie, who accompanied me to Lebanon in 1982; and loving friends from my years in London—they know who they are.

Prologue

What one remembers of love depends on whether it was blissful or painful; whether it brought fulfillment or anguish. My love for Esther never seemed to fit either category. My wife called it an obsession. Perhaps it was.

I was certain I wouldn't like Esther from the moment I learned about her. I worked as a journalist for Reuters and my Australian cousin had given my name to a young woman who wanted to become a writer. I always found doing such favors annoying. I had a slightly jaundiced view of the profession, and though the work was just right for me, I had a hard time encouraging others. My position would no doubt impress a twenty-year-old girl. I was twenty-five—an age difference back in 1951 that made me feel superior and sophisticated. I was also a bit pompous. I was angry that Stephen had bandied my name and phone number about so freely, and made a mental note to write and tell him so.

In reaction to Esther's strong Australian accent over the telephone, I rather overdid my best

BBC-style voice. I hoped to intimidate her so that she'd apologize for disturbing me, and just replace the receiver. But she hardly seemed to notice. I had no choice but to invite her to my Fleet Street office. My plan was to spend an obligatory thirty minutes discouraging her from a writing career and send her on her way.

I knew my attitude was bad; still, it was appropriate to my line of work. Journalism had always been a cynical, cutthroat profession. It suited me, however, providing a full-time education in the social, economic and political life of any place where news erupted.

Before Esther's call I had just finished editing correspondents' reports for the day. Our man in Jerusalem was covering the assassination of Jordan's King Abdullah. A twenty-one-year-old had been sent to do the job by one of the king's rivals, and when the king's own guard shot and killed the assassin "on the spot"—from a journalist's standpoint—I could file it all away as "end of story."

Being a reporter and editor was also demanding. I never knew when I had to work, or where I'd suddenly be sent. I was continually on call which made it hard to have a personal life. But I was hooked; printer's ink, it seemed, ran through my veins.

However, whenever young people came to me for career advice I tended to dissuade them. Giving up a real life for this one was not exactly something I wanted to sell to them or to this young woman. I truly believed I'd be saving her from a life of disillusionment and probable failure. In our brief conversation on the telephone I'd formed a mental image of a naive girl with a bit of literary talent who should probably work for a woman's magazine, get married, and live happily ever after.

I sat back in my "executive" leather chair and surveyed my office. Not much larger than a cubicle, it was still quite impressive for someone who didn't even have a senior position. The interior decorator had also given me an impressive red leather "client" chair—people seemed to feel good in it. My desk was cluttered enough to give an impression of hectic activity, even though I'd already filed my reports for the day and had little to do for the moment. It wasn't unlikely that some unexpected event would change all of that. On my plate for tomorrow was a follow-up story about the ten political murders in the last six years in the Middle East.

Although it was only 3 P.M., London got dark early in winter and I could see my reflection in the window almost as clearly as in a mirror. I straightened my tie and smoothed my dark hair, hoping Esther wouldn't notice the spot I'd developed on my chin; it seemed ridiculous still to be plagued by occasional teenage acne at the advanced age of twenty-five. Fortunately, I was wearing a nice Harris tweed jacket—a birthday present from my mother—with leather elbow patches. I had to admit it gave me that "man about town" look, which provided some distraction from those nasty little spots.

Esther knocked once, then not so much entered as burst in, quite breathlessly. "The lift took a long time coming, so I got impatient and raced up the stairs," she explained, and collapsed into the chair without even seeming to notice its expensive red leather. Her shoulder-length hair was scattered about her face. She pulled it back and patted it down in a reflexive gesture of pulling herself together, but one stubborn lock kept falling over her eyes. "Oh, I'm Esther," she added. "You can call me Essie."

I found myself laughing inside at her wild entrance, though I couldn't tell if it meant I was dealing with a wild woman or a deeply determined one. She was already difficult to read.

"Very well then, Essie, what can I do for you?" I asked in my most official voice, trying to quickly establish a more professional tone to the interview.

"You know, I don't really like the name Essie," she said quite unpredictably. "It's not quite me. I'd rather be called something exotic like Crystal, or Desiree, or Jasmine—but Esther's my name. Have you ever felt that way, like you're not the person you know you were meant to be?"

She wasn't the typical interview, and she continued to draw out different reactions in me. I was torn between thinking her a bit foolish, while at the same time feeling moved by something about her. Was her impetuousness a product of fear and nervousness or a certain sense of conviction about being utterly herself? I watched her, still wondering about this, as she walked around my office carefully reading the text of the journalism awards I'd won and framed. She moved slowly through the room looking at everything, eagerly lifting up magazines and newspapers strewn about the office that had some pieces I'd written in them. Her journey finally landed her back at my desk from which she lifted a small sculpture of *The Thinker*. She turned it around thoughtfully. "I wonder what he's thinking?" She laughed.

Without missing a beat she switched gears, turned to me and asked, "Do you love your work?"

I felt a bit uncomfortable being placed on the spot like that. Fortunately, she didn't wait for an answer but rushed ahead, talking about her own hopes. "I've always dreamed of coming to London to write for a great newspaper. How exciting to be an observer, to participate in the world in that way. That's where I want to to be, in the world. I realize you can't give me a job, after all you just work here, too, but I mean—I hope—you'll give me some contacts, help me get started, and so on. I'll do the rest," she concluded confidently.

Esther looked the epitome of the girl-next-door. She was barely five feet tall. She had a sprinkling of freckles on her nose and dimples in her cheeks, and there was a certain restlessness to her which seemed to be given away by that lock of hair that kept falling into her face. But her dark brown eyes had a certain sparkle. She wasn't beautiful at all, yet her ready spirit, her unpretentious self-determination made her deeply compelling, leaving the girl next door in the dust.

"So tell me more about yourself Essie," I asked, a bit uptight. "You've come so far. What . . ." Once again Essie interrupted me with her rapid train of thoughts, and began to describe her remarkable six-week journey by ship from Australia to England.

She was certainly an adventuress at all of twenty years old. In preparing to tell me her story, she curled her legs up under her skirt and leaned toward me, speaking from someplace in her imagination.

"We went through the Suez Canal and saw Stromboli erupting. Can you imagine? It was absolutely extraordinary. And in Bombay I bought a bottle of Chanel No. 5, only they'd filled it with something awful." She held her cheeks as she laughed. "It smelled like Canal No. 5. We were in Aden, too, right on the equator . . . so hot and horrible. There were women in cages. I couldn't believe my eyes. But no sooner did we see such horrors than we moved on to Marseilles, which I so loved. It was so French!" Her descriptions came in gusts, without any sense of order, but I could see it all through her eyes and in the turns of her expressive hands.

"I slept on deck when it got hot," she confided, "because I was in a ten-berth cabin in the bowels of the ship. We were carrying a cargo of wool which somehow got wet and smelled awful. But the Indian Ocean was beautiful, so vast, with sunsets like symphonies. And then there was the Bay of Biscay which was terrible—rough all the way. I got sick and so did everyone else." She leaned back, laughing, remembering it all.

"Though it sounds terribly exciting, it must have been quite horrible at times," I suggested. I wasn't quite sure how to respond to her, I was so intrigued.

"Actually not. It was wonderful, the best holiday—make that the only holiday—I've ever had. We played deck tennis and had ice cream every day; the flavor was called 'pistachio.' It was green with bits of red maraschino cherry in it, and it was delicious. We listened to concerts and went to parties. Oh, and every day at five, the band on deck played Gershwin and Irving Berlin. It was just splendid!"

I was getting used to her accent. Somehow it didn't sound so terrible; in fact, it was rather nice. She was so spirited, so smart. She had enormous presence for someone so small. Suddenly, I felt very excited about her. I really did want to help her, although she'd endowed me with much more power than I had. I'd got my own job more through good luck than good management; my journalism degree meant much less than the fact that my uncle was on the city desk at the *Daily Telegraph* and just happened to have some good friends at Reuters.

Once I'd gotten the job, I took it seriously. I was proud of my work, although as a typical Englishman

I often downplayed its importance. I knew what
Essie meant about feeling connected to the world
through reporting. I, too, had felt her eagerness,
though now mine was tempered by experience
which brought compromise and some disillusion.
But her passionate nature reawakened something I
liked in myself but with which I had somehow lost
touch. Maybe I wouldn't reprimand Stephen after
all. Maybe I'd write and thank him. I'd only known
Esther for half an hour, but already I was smitten.

*T*he summer of 1952 was perhaps the most vivid one of my life. I remember it as "the summer of Esther." Without my help, Esther found a job just by answering an ad in the paper. She went for an interview and, I suppose, bowled them over—as she had me—with her quick wit and ready spirit. I was thrilled it wasn't a newspaper office, but rather an advertising agency in the West End run by a woman. "Maybe she'll have a real life after all," I thought.

The only writing Essie would be doing would be advertising copy, but it didn't seem to worry her. "Right now as long as I'm writing I don't care if it's just recipes using peanut butter. Anyway, I plan to do lots of real writing in my spare time." I was relieved—though I understood the pull of journalism—that she'd be working in a slightly more "normal" world and would have time to devote herself to other things. I wasn't sure if Essie was over her infatuation with the reporter's life and its promise of engagement with the issues of the day. Only time would tell.

Though Essie talked of having spare time, in reality she had little of it, and I was glad that I was part of the reason. When she wasn't working, we were exploring London together, visiting art galleries and museums, bookshops, and out-of-the-way places where few tourists go. And we spent far too much time just throwing darts in a local pub close to where she lived. Essie shared a flat—just a room, really—with another Australian girl she'd met on the boat to England. Ruth was an artist, very serious and quite pretty, who worked in a graphic design studio. They became close, so close that I became a bit jealous of the jokes and intimacies they shared.

Still, the time Essie and I spent together was heavenly. When Ruth wasn't home, we'd sometimes dance late into the night to the music of Radio Luxembourg. We'd cook together on the primitive gas burner. Some meals were a disaster, but it didn't seem to matter much. What mattered was how close we were becoming. In winter, we'd put a shilling in the gas meter and toast muffins and our toes while we tried to solve the problems of the world. I was falling in love with her, but I knew little about her feelings for me.

We were both Jewish in a world that was largely not. I thought this would bring us even closer to each other. Though I wasn't a "practicing" Jew, I was raised with some tradition. My mother kept a kosher home and lit candles on the Sabbath. When I suggested to Essie that we go to synagogue together, although normally I didn't go either, her reaction was quite hostile.

"I've given it up," she said brusquely.

"What do you mean? You haven't converted, have you?" I asked, horrified.

"No, of course not, but I have a lot of opinions about religious life. You see, my mother did the Sabbath bit, too, but it was a meaningless ritual, and mostly I felt restricted by it. I wasn't allowed to go out Friday night. I wasn't allowed to date boys who were not Jewish; which eliminated 95 percent of the boys I met. Mum and Dad always argued about which traditions mattered and which did not. They didn't know why we lit candles or drank wine. It was awful. I kept waiting for something spiritual to come of it all, but it only felt empty and imprisoning. All that came of it were all the 'thou shalt nots' in my life. I feel uncomfortable about this, but it's the truth.

"In society, being Jewish has always been a terrible burden to me; it stopped me from doing so many things I wanted to do. At school I was the only Jewish child among five hundred pupils. I was supposed to be excused from gentile religious instruction every week, but I went anyway, without telling my parents. I didn't want to be different. There weren't any Jewish day schools in Melbourne then, so even if they could have afforded one, all the private schools were affiliated with churches— Methodist Ladies College, Presbyterian Ladies College, and so on. I went to a state school and tried to pretend I was the same as everyone else. In fact, I even won first prize for religious instruction, a New Testament bound in white calf."

"What did you do with it?"

"Well, I couldn't take it home. I was only eight and terrified. I walked right to the end of the St. Kilda pier, threw it into the ocean, and made a bargain with God."

"What kind of bargain?"

"That if He would not wash it up on shore—it had my name on it—I wouldn't lie anymore about not being Jewish."

"Did it work?" I was taken with her story.

She sighed. "My parents never found out, if that's what you mean. And it wouldn't have helped if I lied or not, all the kids knew I was different. I used to think I had the 'mark of Cain' on my forehead. I applied for a position on a newspaper after I matriculated. I knew I was the best candidate, but you had to fill out a personal profile, including your religion. They gave the job to another girl in my class. She couldn't write at all, but she was a nice safe Protestant."

Then she brightened. "Anyway, if I'd been chosen for the job I wouldn't be here, would I? It was all for the best." I wondered if she had made her peace with this issue or was just putting the best face on it. Still, she had an undeniable resilience I greatly admired.

"It's certainly been best for me. What about you, Essie? Are you happy to be here, with me?" I asked, hoping to coax a word out in my favor. I gently reached out to touch her face. Her eyes smiled.

"I'm so glad you're in my life, Max." But that was all she said, and slowly she slipped her face from beneath my hand.

There was no special man in Essie's life, I knew that. She didn't seem to be looking for love; she had too many plans for that. She was different from the other women her age I knew. She wanted to do things in the world; she was restless for experience, far from ready to settle down. I was certain that she hadn't been intimate with a man yet, even though in every other way she was so open, such a free spirit. I'd had many intimate relationships by then. I could walk away from the others, and sometimes still remain friends, but I couldn't imagine ever letting Essie go; that is, if ever she could be possessed in any way. But she couldn't. She was like quicksilver. I could no more hold on to her than to a snowflake.

I took what pleasure in Essie I could while she was close. We went to the theater, ballet and concerts when I could afford to. But the truth was she was just as happy to line up for two hours with her friends to buy two-shilling tickets in the "gods," the upper dress circle of the theater. She loved the "buskers," the street entertainers. Essie talked to everyone she met; she seemed to want to know everyone in the world. She was dying to speak to the performers, but they never took a break. "They're amazing people, aren't they? Just able to perform wherever there's an audience. They're so free, and yet they know where they belong." Her curiosity was one of her great strengths, and yet it belied her anxieties about how to live her own life; as if she were always asking herself, "Where do I belong?" It was difficult to put together this sense of displacement with the person whose spirit was so alive, so present, and so powerful. I couldn't believe Essie felt so lost.

Essie had a great capacity for pleasure, and not for the things money could buy. In fact, she was probably the least materialistic person I knew. Whenever I tried to buy her a gift she'd grab my arm and pull me away. "I don't need that. But you are so sweet to me, Max, just don't . . ."

I gathered that her family was quite poor, as she only seemed to have the money she earned from her job, and that barely covered her rent and food. She had two "good" dresses, neither of which suited her particularly, especially not the blue one. She should have worn autumn shades—gold, apricot, green, russet—in those she would have blossomed. But she obviously had no money for beautiful clothes, which was perfectly fine with her. She enjoyed dressing up and going to the Savoy when once I blew a week's wages to take her there, but she had just as much fun playing a game of darts and sipping a glass of apple cider at our pub.

Essie preferred to accept gifts that people made for her with their own hands. Poems, paintings and ceramics from friends were her most treasured possessions. On her twenty-first birthday I made her a giant kite. I wasn't at all adept with my hands, but my dad had taught me how to make and fly kites, and I knew having one would thrill her. When I gave it to her she threw her arms around me, wrapping them around my neck like a child, and she planted a kiss on my cheek. That kiss put me in mind of a poem I'd once had to learn at school. It was by a seventeenth-century poet, James Hunt. It began, "Jenny kissed me when we met" and ended:

> *Say I'm weary, say I'm sad;*
> *Say that health and wealth have missed me;*
> *Say I'm growing old but add—*
> *Jenny kissed me!*

"Max, it's wonderful!" she cried. She smiled as she held the kite up in mock flight. "I've always wanted a kite. How did you know? When can we fly it?"

We planned a picnic and kite-flying expedition early one Sunday morning. If I close my eyes, I can relive the beauty of the day. Rotten Row, in Hyde Park, was full of red-coated, jodhpured riders on shiny mares and little boys sailing boats on the Serpentine. We raced across the grass, laughing together, the sun creating golden highlights in her brown hair that streamed behind her as the kite sailed up into the cloudless blue sky. Finally we collapsed breathlessly near the statue of Peter Pan. I felt as if I were living in some romantic movie; I could almost hear the soundtrack in the background. In fact, there was a soundtrack, it came from the musicians who played somewhere nearby in the park.

And Essie, oh Essie. She was like Peter Pan, a rare combination of woman and child. I laughed at her. "You are incredible. I feel so young when I'm with you. And I'm not even embarassed to act so silly together. Imagine that—me, Max, the cynic."

"Not my Max." She smiled knowingly.

I had felt older than my years and kind of cynical before I met her. Maybe it was the people I came into contact with through my work—politicians, sometimes criminals, notable people who had risen to the top, often through unscrupulous methods. But Essie was wholly other. Now that I knew her better, she undoubtedly had the curiosity about people and the world that make a good journalist. Yet it was hard to imagine her as a "tough" reporter encountering corruption firsthand, even though she never shied away from reality. In a way she was tough, despite her open, tender nature.

"Essie, I care for you so much," I suddenly heard myself murmur.

She bent down and picked a blade of grass, studying it intently, deliberately avoiding my eyes.

"And I care for you, Max. You must know that." She tried to make me laugh, but when she saw that I wanted a real response, she became very intense. "Please, Max, don't talk about us. I can't. I just don't know enough about myself to be with someone. Sometimes I feel so lost. And then there are other times where I feel that there are so many things I want—and need—to do before settling down. That is, if I ever settle down. I want to travel, to live in different countries, and to write. Most of all, to write. It's all so painful and confusing. Please, Max, don't feel bad. I need you. It's not you I cannot rest with; it's my life. I want so much . . ."

"Essie, do you think I would really hold you back? We can share our experiences. I would never take away your freedom. I want you to write." I was almost shouting, as if by doing so I could break through that awful wall that separated us.

She was silent for a while. "I don't know who I am yet, Max. I'm so confused about so many things. My Jewishness is part of it. I know I never talk about it, because I can't. I feel like I'm searching for something, but I don't know what it is. I feel this kind of hollowness inside me. Until I know who I am and what I want—and it might take years—I'm not ready to fall in love."

I was devastated. Lying next to her on the blanket, she felt so close. How could I not know the confusion she lived with? I wanted to understand, to help her. I thought my love would do that, but apparently it wasn't enough.

She was right. It did take years, and the yearning was for something neither of us ever expected. But when she found it, it meant I had lost her.

*E*very memory I have of the summer of 1952
revolves around Essie. I must have done other
things, but somehow all I can recall is our being
together. Wherever she invited me I went, no matter what I might have otherwise planned. And when
I was not seeing her I was in agony worrying about
what she was doing and with whom. Obviously we
couldn't be together all the time.

One night she called and said she had a week's
holiday from work and wanted to go to Devon and
Cornwall, which she'd never visited. My holidays
weren't due for another four months, but if necessary I would have invented an attack of bubonic
plague if it was the only way to be with her.
Fortunately, there was no problem.

I'd bought an old London taxi before I met her,

and this was my chance to see if it would actually get us anywhere. Essie loved the idea, and suggested we leave Sunday morning at six. Even that didn't dampen my ardor. I, who hadn't been aware that there was a time such as six o'clock in the morning, was up and running.

I fantasized about what would happen between us on this trip, even though I knew my fantasies would remain just that—fantasies. Still, it was a chance for intimacy away from other people and the pressures of work. The old taxi behaved beautifully. Essie wasn't much of a navigator, which surprised me, given her great independence. But it didn't matter much where we were as long as we were together. We wandered around a little fishing village, wending our way through its tiny cobbled streets. We stopped at the pier where old fishermen in ancient jerseys sat mending fishing nets. I went off to get us some ice cream, and when I returned I watched her from the distance. There she was, that same lock of hair falling into her face, as she talked animatedly to the fishermen, gesturing wildly as she spoke. She was full of questions. She was so hungry to grow, to be engaged with life. I had visited the area many times, but it was only now—with Essie—that it all felt so alive.

The main thing that I remember were the evenings we spent in the fishing village of Mousehole. We stayed at a pub called The Lobster Pot. Even though it was summer, at night there was a blazing log fire. I'd sit on the sofa in front of the fire and Essie would sit on the floor, her head resting on my knee. I think it was in *Rebecca* that the heroine said that she wished you could bottle memories like perfume and whenever you wanted remove the stopper and live them all over again. I don't need to do that, I just have to close my eyes and the scene comes back to me. I can see again the burnished highlights in Essie's soft brown hair, feel again the gentle pressure of her head against my knee, and once more experience the longing to take her into my arms.

While we looked into the fire, Essie would find images in the flames and point them out to me till I could see them myself. Out of each image she spun a tale. Her imagination was vivid. You could see the young writer, always inventing, always observing and commenting on everything she thought about, on everything she saw. When it became late, we walked together to her door to say goodnight.

"I really don't want this night to end at the door," I said, holding her close.

From the pressure of her arms around my neck, I

knew she didn't want it to end either, but for her there was no alternative. Eventually she pulled away with a kind of reluctant sigh. This became our nightly pattern. I didn't want to force the issue and threaten the closeness we had. I knew how to be patient.

We returned to London full of each other. It seemed that nothing could destroy our present joy. But a phone call from Essie's sister did just that. "She's dead," Essie sobbed into my shoulder. "My mother is dead. She had a heart attack. I can't believe it. I just can't believe it. How could she be gone? I loved her so much, Max; she always believed in me, she always believed I would become a writer. Who will I show my stories to now? I won't be able to speak to her ever again. I just can't . . . Who will I talk to? My mother, my own mother." She was bereft.

Essie's family flew with the coffin to bury her mother in Jerusalem. "I don't understand it," she kept repeating, "when she was alive, she hardly talked about Israel. She must have told Dad she wanted to be buried on the Mount of Olives. But why would she want that?"

I didn't know the answer. It must have been terribly expensive for a family who obviously had little money to raise enough to carry out her mother's last wish, but somehow they did. Although Essie had told me that her parents argued a great deal, it now seemed that the loss was unbearable for her father. At the last moment I decided to go with her as well. Reuters had an office in Jerusalem, and I was able to wangle an assignment there for three weeks. Essie was so grateful, and I was glad to be there for her.

The funeral was heart-wrenching. Except for her father and two sisters, we knew no one else, and the Chevra Kadisha, the Jewish Burial Society, called in strangers to make the required *minyan* of ten men. It was difficult to watch the body being lowered into the ground without a coffin, which is Israeli custom. I was horrified. I don't know how Essie survived the ordeal.

On a barren hill among the tombstones we stood listening to the Hebrew incantations. The wind cut through us like a knife, and Essie's shoulders trembled. Below us, the Old City of Jerusalem loomed, a powerful, ancient presence; a silhouette of turrets, minarets and domes.

The only comfort I took from the trip was in help-ing the family, who had little knowledge of Jewish customs, make their way through the burial and the grieving. They decided that they wanted to sit *shiva*, the seven days of mourning, even though they barely knew what that meant. I organized every-thing for them in their hotel room. I covered the mirrors and pictures and arranged low stools for them to sit on. As they knew no one in Jerusalem, few came to visit during the week, except for the people the rabbi had sent bearing food and their sympathies. It was a thoroughly miserable week, and the family was relieved to return to Australia. I was only afraid they would try to persuade Essie to go back with them, but it was never mentioned in my presence. Her father would live with one of the mar-ried sisters, and he seemed resigned to the fact that Essie would be going back to London—at least for a year or two.

After the shiva ended I had another two weeks in Jerusalem and I persuaded Essie to remain as well. It was probably the biggest mistake of my life.

During the day I was busy with my work and Essie spent her time walking around Jerusalem. Every day she fell more and more in love with the ancient holy city. The Promised Land. Indeed, who wouldn't fall

in love with the hilltops and valleys of this breathtaking mountain setting, with its golden light, its
stones as old as time turned into rooftops, ruins and
towers? Jerusalem was unique among all cities, a col-
lision of past and present, of the spiritual and the
practical. Who could not fail to feel the pull of this
historic city rising up out of the desert? I could
imagine Essie overcome by the landscape, by its
ancient and modern people, a place so haunted by
the past. I imagined her walking through the colorful bazaars, past the pungent spice stores, maybe
stopping to look at the shoddy jewelry and embroidered dresses, called *djellabah*. I knew Essie would
love the primitive handmade clothing so suited to
her nature. But when she came home she told me
what moved her the most, and, in a sense, I wasn't
surprised. She spoke of Judaism's most holy ancient
site, the Western or "Wailing" Wall, the Kotel.
Indeed, for thousands of years, this remaining wall,
a ruin from the Second Hebrew Temple destroyed
by the Romans in 70 B.C.E., has been a pilgrimage
site for Jews. Few places can compare to this holy
wall where, pressed between the cracks of its huge
stones, lie hundreds of thousands of pieces of tiny
crumpled paper on which prayers and incantations
to God have been written.

"When I go to the Wall I don't say any prayers," Essie would tell me, "I just stand there, my forehead pressed against the stones. But I am so moved by it all. When I'm at the Wall I feel serene, as if I've come to a place where I was meant to be. I feel whole. All around women pray, and they are alien to me, yet I feel a certain inexplicable kinship. I just stand there and touch the ancient stones while holy services take place all around me. I don't feel the need to say anything. I feel at peace. Sometimes I cry, though I don't know why."

"You're still mourning your mother," I said quietly.

"It's more than that," she insisted. "I feel like I've come home. I feel so connected here. I can't explain it to myself."

In the evenings, Essie and I would take the bus to Tel Aviv. Though I loved Jerusalem, was even moved by it, I felt much more at home in Tel Aviv among the cafés and the cosmopolitan life. Essie would join me wherever I wanted to go, but part of her always stayed in Jerusalem.

One night on the bus going back I fell asleep. When I awoke Essie was writing on the back of an envelope. She didn't want to show me what she had written, but when I insisted, she handed it to me. It

was a poem, the first of many, and as I read it my
heart sank:

> It was not for long
> I left you
> But each parting
> Is a small death
> Now I am returning
> To leafy arms of pine,
> A kiss of sunshine—
> Gold on gray stone.
> The sighing wind
> Whispers secrets to me
> Jerusalem's perfume
> Is my embrace.
> I have missed you . . .
> Missed your gentle blessing.
> But now I am returning—
> Coming home!

I was losing her.

*I*t wasn't even a surprise when the bottom fell out of my world. Essie and I were walking hand-in-hand in the Jerusalem Forest. The path meandered under a canopy of trees, mostly pines, that sighed when the wind ruffled their branches. "We have to remember to confirm our flight back to London; it's only two more days," I reminded her.

"Max, I don't know how to say this. I know you'll be upset, but I'm not going back, I cannot bear to leave Israel yet."

I tried to swallow the giant lump in my throat. "Not coming back to London? But I thought you loved London."

"Yes, I do. You know that. But I always felt somehow like a tourist there, enjoying the theaters and the countryside. I was a spectator. After being in

Jerusalem I know what it feels like really to belong to a place, to feel connected. The landscape is somehow so close to my heart. It feels like me."

I couldn't control the anger my pain was causing. "Essie, that's ridiculous," I blurted out. "How can it feel so right when you don't even speak the language? You can't even connect with the people."

"But I do, on a different level. You see I've always felt like an outsider in my life, like someone pressing their nose against the window watching a party to which they weren't invited. In London, I was almost accepted, but I didn't feel like I really fit in."

"I remember asking you once if you felt a special bond to the Jewish people and you said no."

"I was wrong," she said simply.

"Essie, losing your mother has been devastating for you, I realize that. I don't want to drag in a lot of psychological jargon, but I think your feelings are coming out in the wrong way. Maybe you're trying to bring your mother back by remaining in Israel and identifying yourself more as a Jew. . . . What I mean," I insisted, "is that identifying oneself from a religious standpoint is not consistent with the Essie I know."

I was desperately trying to hold on to her and said anything that came into my head, though I believed what I was saying was true. "You're just fascinated by the novelty of it. Israel is a harsh country, too abrasive for Westerners. It'll break you."

"Leaving it would break me," she said emphatically.

"But how will you live, what will you do? You don't have money, you can't speak the language, you don't have a job. You won't survive!"

For a few minutes, the old Essie came back. She squeezed my hand and laughed, a bit awkwardly I thought. "I can do it, Max. I know you'll be angry when I tell you this, but please try to hear it from my point of view."

I was afraid of what was coming.

"One day in Tel Aviv I found the office for kibbutz volunteers. They have this program, you work for six hours in the fields or the kitchens or the children's house, and in return you have a place to live, free meals and an Ulpan, a school where they teach you Hebrew. Max, why don't you stay, too?"

"I'm a Londoner," I said despairingly. "I'm not a likely candidate to milk cows and grow artichokes."

"You could work for Reuters," she suggested.

"But I wouldn't see any more of you than if I go back to London. People work six days a week in this mad country and the buses don't run on the Sabbath."

"Max, don't be angry. Let me try it for six months."

"I don't want to lose you on an insane whim."

What we both knew was that you can't lose what you never had.

I went back to London. Essie stayed in Israel.

$\mathcal{E}$ssie's kibbutz was only forty minutes from Jerusalem, on the old Latrun Road. She said she'd try it for six months; the truth is I didn't think she'd last six days. Even if she didn't miss me, she'd miss the intellectual life of Fleet Street and the promise of her journalistic career. One night in London I took her to see the *Daily Telegraph* put to bed. I'll never forget her absolute fascination. When the great presses began to roar, she laughed like a child. "Isn't that the most amazing sight? This great machine spewing out the latest news—and all while everyone's fast asleep. Soon it will be at everyone's doorstep, informing their day. They'll talk about it to their colleagues, to their friends and neighbors." She wasn't just talking for effect, either. Essie never did. She was truly moved by what she saw.

Like I said, given her love of engaging with world events, I didn't think she'd last in that tiny village of the kibbutz. As always, I was wrong, and I knew it from the first letter she sent me.

Dearest Max,

It's so difficult to write. With every sentence I imagine you angry or recoiling from the world I've embraced. It may not be fair, but I need to share this with you, because you know me. Yet I don't want to hurt you or turn you away from me. There is much for me here, Max. I guess I want you to accept that, to convince you. I never expected to be here, to love kibbutz life so much. I've always been a city girl; but I realize I didn't know myself, not in this way.

I'm working harder—physically—than at any time in my life. We go out in the field to pick tomatoes just before sunrise when the light is kind of pearly, almost silver. There we spend six hours squatting on the ground.

At dawn, it's almost impossible to see the tomatoes; they hide under the leaves and you have to feel for them. In the sunlight, each one is like an oil painting, scarlet, round and firm, so perfect, so beautiful. Tomatoes are very cheap in Israel in summer; it hardly seems worth all the labor for the ridiculously low price they bring; but as several of us are volunteers, and the members don't get paid anyhow, it must be profitable.

I've also been studying Hebrew.

I miss Jerusalem, but if I'm not too tired I take a bus in the late afternoon to be there for a few hours just to feel the profound sense of history, see the hills, and watch the people. My kibbutz brother, Adi, takes me up on the tractor or I hitch a ride. I've become part of the Goldfarb family. All volunteers are adopted by a family. There are the parents and three children, including Adi. But more about them later.

I think I forgot to tell you that this is a religious kibbutz. I decided that as I was in Israel I might as well learn as much as I could about being Jewish. I don't know exactly why. Anyway, at least if I decide later to reject it, I'll be making that decision from knowledge, not from ignorance. Does that make sense?

I think what moves me most is the Sabbath, and it's ironic, because, as you know, I hated it as a child. It means so much here, and makes so much sense. Here it's an oasis. Friday afternoon all work stops and the week kind of gently subsides. Everything feels transformed by the Sabbath. It truly feels holy. We fill the

communal dining room with flowers from the garden;
now it's late-blooming roses in white, gold, palest
pink and deep red. The tables are covered with white
cloths, and the loaves of braided challah bread are
put on each table with a bottle of wine. Everything
feels so whole, so right, so purposeful.

Can you understand what this means to me?
Please tell me you do.

Affectionately,
Essie

I dropped the letter on my desk among the pile of
less hurtful correspondence. Her words disturbed
me. The wild enthusiasm she had displayed for
London was more than matched by her kibbutz
experience. Would she throw herself heart and soul
into becoming an Israeli as she'd done at making a
place for herself in London as a writer? I knew
something about her restless soul, and my gut feeling was she was not going to find her peace with me.
And I sure as hell didn't enjoy the references to her
kibbutz "brother" Adi!

*E*very letter that came from Essie heightened my sense of unease. I missed her terribly, but I couldn't feel a corresponding nostalgia for me, although I tried to read between the lines to find some hope. What I did find there were frightening portents. Whenever she referred to something she and Adi had done together, like taking a trip to Jerusalem or teaching her how to drive, I grew fearful of a budding romance. Sometimes in desperation I would drop in on her friend Ruth in the hope she might have had a letter with more information about what Essie was really feeling. Another girl had taken over Essie's share of the small apartment, and even though the salon was strewn with their belongings, I could still feel Essie's presence in the way different ornaments and pictures had been arranged, the jaunty angle of the cushions she had bought and placed on the dilapidated sofa with the sagging springs. Whenever she earned a bit of extra money Essie would spend it at the flea market on interesting objects, baskets, brass candlesticks. She had a wonderful eye for shape, texture, and color. It hurt me to go to the apartment, but I couldn't stay away.

Ruth missed her as much as I did. We'd read each other's letters, and I felt sad that there was nothing private enough in mine to preclude other eyes seeing them. Essie wrote me long and affectionate missives, but they could have been to a brother or a cousin of whom she was particularly fond. To Ruth, she wrote in more detail about her increasing interest in Judaism. As she had rightly guessed, my response would not be very enthusiastic. The truth was I didn't want anything about Essie to change. I wanted her always to be the way I remembered her, tough but fragile, excited by things others would take for granted, always curious, always searching, serious but a little naive. I didn't want anything to alter her spontaneity. Being religious would be such a heavy burden; I was afraid it would make her too solemn.

Eight months had passed since Essie had left London. When the six months' "trial period" at the kibbutz came to an end, she didn't even mention leaving. In the early months she continued to be fascinated by my descriptions of London and Fleet Street, and I sensed in her a thirst for information. But as time passed she barely responded to my news and instead sent me pen portraits of her life in glowing terms:

It is autumn now . . . brisk, chilly mornings but sunny days and sunsets in scarlet, gradually changing to indigo. The tomatoes are long finished and I'm working now in the vineyard. Although it is the end of the season, we are still picking grapes, big purple clusters of California Flame, and the seedless sweet green grapes known as Thompson's Sultanina. I eat as many as I pick, the juice is like ambrosia, and the grapes are so plump and firm. Nothing gets wasted at the kibbutz, even the leaves are served in the dining room stuffed with rice and pine nuts.

Our synagogue, Beit Knesset, is beautiful. It's so open that birds fly in and out during the service. I listen to the cadences of the Hebrew words rising and falling, and look outside to see fields and trees and sheaves of wheat. Nothing seems more natural here than to worship the Creator.

Adi usually reads the Torah portion. Over lunch

we discuss the commentaries. Now I understand how scholars can sit in a Yeshiva for their whole lives and continue learning day after day. The Torah is really a commentary on all of life. When I see how relevant these ancient texts are to contemporary life, I am filled with awe at the wisdom they contain. Instead of superstition and tradition, as I once viewed these biblical stories, they now engage my intellect and I am moved by their meaning.

Adi's family, the Goldfarbs, are very warm people, and have made me feel so welcome. I still miss my mother more than I can say, but visiting her grave in Jerusalem comforts me; I feel her close by. The sense that Jerusalem is home never leaves me, even though I am very content just now at the kibbutz.

By the way, I wrote a short story about life on the kibbutz and sent it to the BBC. They accepted it! You can imagine how thrilled I am. Please be proud of me, too, Max. My first published work. It's being broadcast on the twenty-fourth of next month. I'm not sure what time. I hope you will listen.

Love,
Essie

I did listen, and I found my cheeks wet with tears. It was good, very good, but I knew it would be. What

I wasn't prepared for was her voice behind every word, loving her life. The story was a celebration of life, but a life that I wasn't sharing. I had never before felt so alone and so bereft.

It was the beginning of spring when I decided it was time to go to Israel. This time I took two weeks vacation and determined not to go near the Reuters office. I wrote to ask Essie if I could come; her enthusiastic response buoyed me from the pain of our separation:

Dear Max, of course you can! I am so delighted. You can even have your own cottage. It won't be the King David, but you'll be comfortable. Of course, you'll have to abide by the laws, the Halacha—*no smoking on Shabbat, or turning lights on and so on, but you already know all the rules. I have saved up quite a bit of vacation time, so we can have a lot of fun, maybe even go to Eilat for some sun!*

Taking a trip with Essie filled me with hope and anticipation. I pictured us on isolated coral beaches dotted with palm trees. I felt that if I could ever win her back it would be there.

Essie met me at the airport; she had learned to drive and had borrowed one of the kibbutz cars. She looked even lovelier than I remembered. She seemed to stand straighter and taller than before, which gave her small frame more weight and dignity. Her brown eyes, too, looked more intense. She wore a simple cotton blouse and a skirt of pale apricot and burnt orange, and the endearing sprinkling of freckles on her nose over her deep suntan stood in delightful contrast to this greater seriousness. The joy she expressed upon seeing me seemed genuine, and it moved me beyond words.

She drove well, although the highway seemed to be full of suicidal maniacs intent on killing themselves and us. I found myself clutching the edge of the dashboard, my knuckles turning white, as taxis overtook us, sometimes from the wrong side, and cars wove in and out, changing lanes at will and without giving signals. Every now and then, drivers would stick their heads out of their windows and yell epithets at each other. What amazed me was that Essie seemed to find this behavior quite normal.

Despite this, we arrived in good time at the kibbutz, and parked the car outside my cottage. I was
touched that she'd placed a big bowl of fruit and a
vase of flowers on the table. The room was filled
with the perfume of freesias, hyacinths and wild violets which she'd picked herself.

I desperately wanted to be alone with her, but was
saddened when she told me we would be eating at
the Goldfarbs. "They are so anxious to meet my
friend from London," she pleaded, "because they
know how much I care about you." I winced at the
word *care*, it fell so short of what I wanted her to feel.

I felt terribly uncomfortable at dinner from the
first moment, when they all, including Essie, ritually
washed their hands and said the special prayer—
motzi—before partaking of the bread. I knew what to
do, that wasn't the point: I couldn't bear seeing
Essie living by someone else's rules and conforming
so unquestioningly. She had been my rebel. I felt
that I was sitting opposite a complete stranger.

Everyone was very hospitable but I felt a certain
distance, and I didn't have to look far for the reason. Adi was obviously in love with Essie. He used
the proprietorial "we" whenever he could, made
asides in Hebrew that excluded me, and found
excuses to continually smile into her eyes. Actually I

found his behavior very childish, and I waited for Essie to show some irritation. She didn't. She laughed at his jokes and returned his smiles. My appetite rapidly left me, and suddenly I felt if I didn't get some air I would choke.

Essie insisted on helping with the dishes before we left. It was 9 P.M. before we finally got away. I felt sullen and ungracious and unreasonably angry at Essie. She obviously sensed it and tried to make amends, slipping her arm through mine.

"Let's take a walk. It's a beautiful evening." We walked across green fields carpeted with red poppies toward the orchards. The night was perfumed with the scent of orange blossoms, and the heavy sensual aroma of magnolias filled me with longing. Slowly my anger slipped away, but there was a deep sadness I couldn't dispel. Finally, I had to ask the question that haunted me all evening.

"Essie, when are you coming back to London?"

"It's difficult to know. Not yet. I was so happy in London, and I do miss it so much. I miss you. But it's different here. What I feel, it's not really happiness, it's a kind of contentment."

I looked away, but as I turned back toward her I asked, "And Adi?"

"What about him?"

"He's in love with you."

She suppressed her reaction, but her face told me more than words.

"Do you love him?"

"I haven't thought about it."

"And I've thought about nothing else since you first started talking about him in your letters."

I waited for her to dismiss him with a laugh, but she didn't.

"He's been very good to me, Max. Really a kind of tutor."

"Yes, I'm sure," I murmured to myself. I hated the way I sounded. Bitter. Resentful.

She looked distressed. "You don't understand. I was so ignorant about everything—faith, tradition . . . I have so much to learn."

"Essie, if that's what you want, I can teach you."

"But you don't practice yourself."

"I could, if it's important to you."

"It wouldn't be the same, because you don't believe in it. I know you understand it all, but faith comes with doing; it's not enough otherwise."

We came to a wooden bench and sat down. The setting was unbelievable. The trees were silhouetted against a starry sky, there was a moon of burnished gold, the air was heavy with night blooming flowers, and here we were discussing Judaism.

"I don't like Adi," I suddenly burst out like a child.

"You're jealous?"

"Of course I'm bloody jealous. What do you expect?"

I put my arm around her. She didn't draw away but she didn't curl into me either. We sat in silence for an interminable length of time. Finally she broke it.

"Max, I . . . I have to go. It's getting late. I usually get up at five!"

She was clearly distressed and beside herself, and I knew she had to get away from me right then.

With Essie I always seemed to take one step forward and two steps back. I accompanied her to her door and returned to my cottage alone.

The following morning, as if nothing had happened the night before, we drove to Eilat by way of the Dead Sea. The farther south we went, the more the scenery resembled a lunar landscape. After we left Jerusalem, on the road to Masada, there was almost no vegetation. The hills were smooth and undulating and the colors—beige, rust, olive and brown—gave it a strange and eerie kind of beauty, lonely and desolate. Despite the heat, I often found myself giving an involuntary shiver when we passed a lone shepherdess leading her flock of black goats across the arid, inhospitable hills or passed a Bedouin encampment of black tents with a camel or two lazing next to them. It felt so biblical. It seemed that somewhere along the way we had lost the twentieth century.

Essie loved it. She spoke in the kind of super-
latives she had used in London at the time we had
both been so happy. I thought it was beautiful, too,
but I didn't want her to fall under its spell.
Everything conspired against my persuading her to
leave Israel, and I saw Eilat and our time alone
together as my last chance.

I couldn't remain impervious to her enthusiasm—
I never could—and soon we were laughing and even
singing together. I always enjoyed that fact that with
her Australian background and my British one, we
knew the same songs and laughed at the same jokes.

When the Dead Sea came into view, we were both
spellbound. The sea was a sheet of crystal, shimmering in the heat, with the mountains of Moab as
a backdrop. Not a ripple disturbed its surface. We
stopped the car and walked to the edge. It was magnificent, otherworldly in its silvery silence. There
was a feeling of timelessness about it that was posi-
tively awe-inspiring, and we found ourselves almost
whispering so as not to disturb the universe.

Not far away a group of tourists were having a
great time swimming in the Dead Sea, covering
themselves with mud, and a few were showing
off, lying in the water reading the newspaper. "You
can't sink," Essie explained, "because of the high

concentration of salt. It keeps you buoyant." I suggested we go in ourselves, but she didn't seem too keen on the idea. After a while we drove on, past the towering fortress of Masada with its tragic history of Jewish heroism and martyrdom, and the strangely shaped rock known as "Lot's Wife." The legend has it that a woman turned into a pillar of salt when she disobeyed God's injunction not to look back on His destruction of the wicked cities of Sodom and Gomorrah. I wondered if Essie felt that looking back on her life in London with me would somehow betray a vow she had made to her new home. It was a weird sensation, not just the fact that we were discussing events that took place thousands of years ago, but that they had somehow come to life and were completely believable. As Essie pointed out, archaeology, rather than disproving the Bible, continually affirmed its truth.

The shadows began to lengthen the farther we drove, becoming a deep indigo as twilight deepened into night. The moon was enormous and the stars almost blue. Essie looked at me and smiled. "This is an enchanted landscape," she said. For some crazy reason I felt compelled to compare it to other magnificent places, just to let her know this wasn't the only wondrous place in the world. "You know"—I turned to her—"if we were driving around the lakes of Scotland, near Loch Ness for instance, under the stars or up in the north of England in Wordsworth country, walking knee-deep in daffodils, it would also seduce our senses." But I only sounded defensive.

This was not the most beautiful scenery in the world, but it had a unique quality of timelessness that I'd never encountered before. An occasional camel silhouetted against the moon, the strange contours of the hills, all somehow separated us from reality. After a while we stopped talking, driving through the night in companionable silence. I don't know what she was thinking about, but I was mentally advancing and discarding tactics to wean her away from this land that seemed to have laid claim to her soul. If she'd wanted to go back and live in Australia, although I'd never been there, I could have dealt with it. I knew I'd be able to work there, relate to the people, talk the language. Even though it was ten times the distance from England that Israel was, it was closer to my sensibility.

Israel could have been on another planet; I found no common denominator with anything I had ever experienced. My Judaism was a comforting tradition like a child snuggling into the warm folds of his father's coat—candles and wine on Friday night, new clothes for Yom Tov, breaking the wine glass under the *chuppah* at a cousin's wedding—those were the rituals I understood. Israel wasn't like that. It was a country of enormous contrasts, with no middle ground where I could feel comfortable. Everyone seemed to be a saint or a sinner, deeply mystical or aggressively earthbound. Where my London friends were journalists or photographers, here the people I met were poets, philosophers and artists. Much of the landscape was primitive, even primeval. Jerusalem was an emotion more than a city. It seemed to hover between earth and heaven. I had only a short space of time to persuade Essie to return to London with me, but I had nothing to offer in exchange for what she'd be leaving. I thought of a poem we'd learned at school:

> *But I, being poor, have only my dreams.*
> *I have spread my dreams under your feet.*
> *Tread softly, for you tread on my dreams!*

The next few days would decide whether Essie would trample them into the dust.

We were registered at the Moon Valley, a kind of motel with individual cabins built around the swimming pool, and a nightclub/bar and dining room forming the hotel part of the accommodation. We had single but adjoining cabins.

To reach our cabin we had to circle the pool, and, to be truthful, I nearly fell in on our way to breakfast the first morning. Stretched out on lounge chairs all the way around lay topless Scandinavian women taking in the sun. This was before the era of the bikini, and I'd never seen so much golden, gorgeous flesh contrasting with flaxen hair and blue eyes in my life!

Essie was very embarrassed. "These are not Israeli girls," she hastened to assure me, "they're tourists from Scandinavia." Since I couldn't pretend I hadn't noticed them, I tried a touch of humor: "This is the way God created women."

She flushed. "I don't appreciate your making glib remarks at the expense of my beliefs."

"And I can't abide your holier-than-thou attitude. You never used to be narrow-minded and judgmental. You were always so interested in people, all kinds of people."

"I guess I've been so removed from all of this. It's hard to bridge these worlds."

I left it at that.

It had been quite late by the time we arrived, registered, and unloaded our luggage, but we weren't tired and decided to walk into town for a late supper.

The summer night was magic. We walked the perfumed streets of Eilat, and the warm air felt like a caress on bare skin. The moon hung like a big golden ball in the starry sky. Floating nightclubs and cafés with their multicolored lights reflected like bright jewels on the water. And out of every doorway laughter and music could be heard—the whole world seemed young and in love. I couldn't believe that this powerful assault on the senses would not have a romantic effect on Essie.

We found a marvelous café on the beach, and ate

mouth-watering grilled fish and salad to the accompaniment of gentle waves lapping at the shore. Strains of "Rhapsody in Blue" found us from a nightclub somewhere off in the distance. "Setting by Gershwin," I murmured, and Essie smiled at me so tenderly my heart lurched. Later we walked along the beach, the lights of Aqaba, in Jordan, twinkling across such a short stretch of water it seemed impossible to believe that enemies could live so close to each other.

We held hands, and, as I recall, uttered few words. It was enough just to be together, away from all pressures, from her boyfriend Adi and from the kibbutz, from having to make any decisions. "Time, we've got time," I kept telling myself.

We kissed goodnight. Her lips felt so warm, so tender. I wanted to linger there, but she gently pulled away; her movement said, "Please don't." I couldn't hold on to what was not mine to have. How could this happen? How could I have let her slip through my fingers? I felt a terrible chill run through my body, as though something was taking leave of my very soul.

The days had been almost perfect, although the nights continued to be lonely. We swam, we visited the underwater museum, we danced, we sunbathed, we even spent a hilarious evening at the floating casino where we both finished with a small profit at the roulette wheel. More than anything else we talked and the bond between us grew stronger and stronger as we came to understand each other better. We were close. I found myself confiding hopes and fears I had never disclosed to another human being and, although I had never believed such a thing possible between a man and woman, Esther really became my best friend. That's not to say there was a lessening of my desire for her, but rather it was deepened by my respect, affection, and, I suppose, the closest word is tenderness.

It wasn't until our last evening in Eilat that I did insist on a decision about her return to London. Just as I had comforted myself at the beginning of the vacation that we had time, as the end drew near, I realized time had run out. We were sitting on the beach, the gently breaking waves the only sound at this deserted spot. The peacefulness of the external world stood in stark contrast to what I was feeling inside. Somehow I knew this evening would decide the direction of the rest of my life.

In my mind I had prepared quite a masterly speech, but when the time came to deliver it I forgot everything and just blurted out: "Essie, what's going to happen to us now?"

"I think it's up to you, Max."

"I want to marry you, Essie."

She didn't pretend to be surprised. "The price might be too high."

"What is the price?"

"I think you know. I want to stay in Israel, and live as an observant Jewish woman."

I took a deep breath. "Essie, can't we compromise? Judaism is about tradition to me. I do what my father does, maybe a bit less than what his father did. But to start keeping kosher, not traveling on Shabbat and so on, would be very hard for me."

She smiled. "You'd have to do a lot more than that."

"Such as?"

"You'd have to care. Judaism would have to matter to you. If we have children, I would want them to have a father who could teach them to love their religion."

I was silent.

"People change, Max."

"Yeah, sometimes not for the better."

"I've found something here in Israel I'd been searching for all my life without knowing it. Can't you understand? Practicing Judaism, finding meaning and spirit in all things, has filled that terrible emptiness inside me, Max. How can I turn away from something that feels so right?"

"Suppose, just suppose, I agreed. Would you marry me and come back to London?"

It was her turn to be silent. I thought she was thinking it over, but all she was doing was trying to find a way to say no. "It's not going to work, is it, Max? I'm staying in Israel. I can't go back to London. It's all part of the same thing for me."

I was so angry I wanted to lash out at anything. "You've been brainwashed by that bloody kibbutz and that Adi who thinks driving a tractor ought to win him a Nobel Prize." I hardly knew what I was saying. "What happened to Esther Goodman the writer, the poet, the girl with all the dreams? You want to bury yourself on some primitive commune and pick tomatoes for the rest of your life? God gave you a talent and you're just going to dissipate it. This makes me sick!"

She was white with anger, too. "You spent one day at the kibbutz and met Adi for an hour. You know nothing about my life. And as far as writing goes, it's not mutually exclusive. I'll still do it. I'll do everything."

"You'll do nothing. You'll only be a housewife."

Suddenly she was crying. Her shoulders were heaving in convulsive sobs. "I'm so sorry, Essie," I whispered. "I'm so sorry." I tried to put my arms around her, but she turned away.

"Why do you have to be intolerant? Do you even care about what this means to me? Do you care about me at all?"

"I do, Essie. If you only knew how much." I felt horrified about how I had treated her.

"Oh Max, I'm so sorry it turned out this way. I'm so sorry and sad, but I can't marry you. If we stayed or if we left, one of us would be filled with resentment and we'd end up hating each other. There's no way to resolve this."

Her words broke my heart. I knew she was right.

I didn't even try to convince her we could work it out, because I realized we couldn't. We didn't talk anymore, we just sat on the beach listening to the waves, but now they sounded like a dirge.

As we walked back to the motel, I told her that there was no point in my going back to the kibbutz with her. I'd leave the next morning from Eilat if I could organize a flight.

"Will we remain friends, Max?"

"Friends?" I repeated absently.

When I got up the next morning I found that Essie had checked out an hour earlier, leaving me a poem:

> *In Parting*
> *The sadness in your heart and mind*
> *Equals the sadness left behind.*
> *I, sad for the selfish reason*
> *That I lose your strong companionship*
> *And cannot choose*
> *From all the others who will stay*
> *One I would have*
> *Replace you for a day.*
> *You, sad for the simple reason*
> *Similar,*

That in your place of future
Far, so far,
You will be searching, too—
For something lost that holds familiar
warmth . . .
Or something new.

It was more than a year before I had any word of Essie. I went back to London, drank a lot more than was good for me, had a series of meaningless affairs, and was leading a rather dissolute life when I ran into Ruth at a party. I was glad to meet her again; she was my only link with Essie. She loved her, too, and the fact that Essie had elected to stay in Israel had also left a void in Ruth's life. We spent most of the evening talking about Essie and reminiscing about her, almost as one would do about a loved one who had died. Ruth still corresponded with her, and brought me up to date on the fact that she was still at the kibbutz, and seemingly very contented.

So it was not quite such a shock to me that one day a large oblong envelope fell out of my mailbox

addressed to me in Essie's easily recognizable writing. It was a wedding invitation. Inside was a short
note:

Dear Max,

*A lot of time has elapsed since we saw each other,
and nothing remains the same. I am sure your life is
also full of events and relationships about which I am
unaware. Please try to be happy for me. This is what
I want and what I need. I don't suppose you will
come to my wedding, but it would give me such joy if
you would. You will always be very special to me.
Think about it.*

Affectionately,
Essie

I read and reread the invitation, which was
printed in Hebrew and in English. I was about to go
out and get drunk when the phone rang. It was
Ruth.

"You met Adi, what's he like?"

"A moron!" I said obnoxiously.

"What's wrong with him?"

"Everything's right with him, that's what's wrong.
He's tall and muscular, and a religious maniac like
she is. He's been in the Israeli army and now he's a

farmer, which in her eyes makes him some kind of saint—you know the thing she's got about putting your hands into the holy soil of Israel. Jesus!"

I knew I was acting like a complete idiot, but I was in pain, and I still couldn't fathom that Essie's life would have turned out this way. It didn't make sense to me. I understood her search, her need to find connection, but I was certain she wouldn't really find what she was looking for in such a restricted world.

"Come with me, Max. We could get a special deal on a charter flight."

"I'll think about it," I said, not intending to go even for a minute. But it was strange; after I hung up the idea kept nagging at me. Maybe if I did see her again, I could lay the ghost. Maybe seeing her joined irrevocably to another man would give me what I needed to put her out of my life. These were the excuses I kept giving myself, but the truth was I had to see her one more time, even as someone else's bride. I was a junkie yearning for a fix. The line kept going through my head: "'Tis better to have loved and lost than never to have loved at all." Despite all the pain, I wouldn't have wanted not to have known her. The Essie I had loved was the girl I had known in London, scintillating, impetuous, ready for anything. She had changed, and maybe seeing her as she was now would free me so I could get on with my life. I was getting sick of my bachelor existence; it was time I had a home and a family, too. Perhaps there was someone else I could love.

So it was that I told Ruth I'd go with her. I spent a lot of time deciding on a wedding present. I couldn't bring myself to give them a gift for their home, or anything that he would share. I remembered that Essie had once mentioned that she loved pearls and I found a perfect pear-shaped one, like a teardrop, on a thin silver chain. The jeweler put it in a blue velvet box lined with white satin. It reminded me of a very fancy coffin—the death of my hopes.

Once we were on the plane, I regretted my decision to go. We flew El Al, and the Israeli music they played as we took off reminded me of my time with Essie in Eilat. Inside I was hurting like hell, but I wisecracked and kidded around with Ruth until I couldn't take it anymore. I had two stiff drinks and pretended to sleep. Ruth squeezed my hand in an understanding way, so I guess I wasn't fooling anyone.

We arrived the day before the wedding. Arrangements had been made for us to stay at the kibbutz. Essie's father and sisters had come from Australia. I shared a cabin this time with her father, and Ruth with her sisters. He seemed a lot frailer than when I'd met him in Jerusalem when his wife died. He greeted me warmly, like a long-lost friend. I think he felt as much an alien in Israel as I did, maybe even more so. We sat down over a cup of coffee before I'd even unpacked.

"I've never forgotten how you helped us when my wife died, Max," the old man said.

"It was nothing, Mr. Goodman. I was happy to be of help."

"You know, Max, I had the idea that you and Essie were keen on each other."

I smiled wryly. "Yes, I was very fond of her."

"And what about her?"

"Not enough to come back to England with me, I'm afraid."

"Oh, so that was the fly in the ointment."

"More or less."

"I would have been happier if she had," he confided. "Ideally, I'd have liked her to come back to Melbourne. I knew Australia didn't tempt her, but she seemed so happy in London. Israel worries me, what with the Arabs and the wars and everything. What do you think of Adi?" he asked abruptly.

I hedged. "Well, I hardly know him. . . ."

"Still, you must have formed some opinion."

"He seems a solid, reliable kind of guy," I managed to say with great effort.

"I hope so." He sighed. "You know, with such a different background, it won't be easy. Sure, she speaks Hebrew now, but the culture is different, it's like transplanting a seed into alien soil and hoping it'll take. He's a handsome boy to be sure, but I can't help wishing it were you."

I managed a paroxysm of coughing to cover up the lump in my throat and made my excuses to retire early. I hadn't even seen Essie yet, but I knew I would see her the next morning. I slept fitfully, waking up every hour or two as if from bad dreams, but not actually remembering them. I cursed myself for having come back to Israel and putting myself through such a trauma.

I had breakfast in the communal dining room and sat with Ruth and Essie's family. None of them looked very happy or excited, although the wedding was to be in eight hours, at 4 P.M. I saw Adi's family, but not Adi, and hoped they would have forgotten me, but Tali—the teenager—spotted me and came racing across to our table. "Max, how wonderful that you came! Do you remember me?"

"Of course. You have grown into a lovely young lady."

She blushed with pleasure. "I'll be sixteen soon. I'm going to be the bridesmaid. I have a superb dress. Not as pretty as Essie's of course, but it's the prettiest one I've ever had."

"I'm sure you'll look great. Your English has improved."

"Yes it has. That's because I spend so much time with Essie, and now she's going to be my sister."

Essie would be her sister now, but who would she be to me? Tears welled up in my eyes as I contemplated Essie finally being severed from my life.

After breakfast I thought I'd take Essie her gift, but I really didn't want to see Adi. I broached the subject gingerly to Ruth. "I suppose Essie is having breakfast with Adi."

"Oh no, she hasn't seen him for a week."

"What do you mean?"

"That's the custom with religious couples, Essie told me. They've just talked on the phone since last Sunday."

For some incomprehensible reason, this made me feel better, and I set off for her cottage with almost a light heart. The sun was shining, the birds were singing, roses were blooming everywhere in a riot of color, and I was about to see the only girl I had ever truly loved. I must have been in a state of delirium. How else could I have even tolerated seeing her?

She had just washed her hair and was drying it with a towel when I arrived. Her hair was hanging in damp tendrils all around her face and she looked so lovely it was hard for me to breathe.

"Max, oh Max, I can't believe it's really you. Come in. It means so much to me that you came. Thank you, Max." She took both my hands and led me inside. I noticed, however, that she left the door ajar.

"Mazel tov," I said awkwardly, at an unaccustomed loss for words. There was an uncomfortable silence and I fished in my pocket for the present. "I bought you a small gift, I hope you like it."

She untied the gold cord carefully and then undid the white and gold paper to reveal the blue velvet box. She looked at it without speaking for several moments and then finally opened it. When she saw the pearl, resting like a teardrop, with its silver chain against the white satin, her eyes filled tears. "It's the most beautiful thing I've ever seen," she whispered.

"I didn't know what to bring; I hoped you'd like it," I mumbled.

"You know me so well," she began, and then I saw that she really was crying.

I couldn't bear it. "My dearest, don't. Don't cry," I said, suddenly finding myself comforting her.

"I'm sorry. It was just a sudden memory of us."

"Essie, are you sure, really sure, this is what you want? To marry Adi and live on a kibbutz for the rest of your life? To stay in Israel forever?"

She raised her eyes slowly to mine. "I've decided, Max. It's what I have to do."

"Do you love him? Are you sure he's right for you?"

"He's a very good man, Max. I've learned so much from him."

"Jesus, we're talking about a husband, not a teacher!" I exploded. "Are you in love with him?"

There was an imperceptible pause. "Yes," she said softly.

"Then that's it. I wish you luck and happiness and—" I couldn't finish the sentence. I was all choked up.

"Max, I love you, too, in a different way. I'll never forget you. What we had together."

I couldn't stand it. "Essie, we never had anything together, that's the tragedy. If we had, you wouldn't be marrying someone else."

"One day there'll be someone for you, too, Max.

And she'll be the luckiest girl in the world, because you're special, very special."

There was nothing more to say. I said good-bye and walked out the door.

I wished I could leave before the wedding took place instead of having to witness her become the wife of another man.

I kept pretty much to myself all day and felt increasingly depressed as the time for the wedding drew near. At 4 P.M. I was still sitting in the cottage gazing moodily through the window when there was a light tap on the door and Ruth came bustling in. "There you are, Max. Let's go, we'll miss the chuppah."

I liked Ruth, and she looked so very attractive in her linen suit and high-heeled pumps. If I hadn't been so besotted with Essie, she might have made a big impression on me. As it was, I just nodded glumly and followed her to a clearing where I got the fright of my life. Essie was wearing a magnificent bridal gown and was seated on the most horrific chair I'd ever seen. It was covered in white net of some kind strewn with wildflowers. "My God, she looks like a sacrifice," I gasped. "Another custom," Ruth whispered. "That's where she receives guests before the wedding. It's a bridal chair. You can go and speak to her and congratulate her."

Ruth obviously didn't know I'd visited Essie that morning and prodded me forward. As it happened, everyone else had moved away and were helping themselves to drinks set up nearby on a trestle table, and she also hurried off to speak to someone. "You look lovely," I said softly.

I noticed she was wearing the pearl pendant, and her hand instinctively moved up to finger it.

"You look pretty handsome yourself." She smiled. I was wearing a three-piece suit, and when I looked around I saw that, apart from her father, I was the only man who was. Even the groom wore an open-necked shirt and blue trousers.

"I feel a bit overdressed," I commented.

"Israelis dress very casually, but it's nice to see that you went to so much trouble," said Essie.

"I always dress up for weddings and funerals," I said bitterly, and then regretted it. "Sorry, Essie."

Just then mad singing broke out and a horde of men, their arms around each other, came dancing toward the bride, with Adi in their midst. I hurriedly moved away.

Adi stepped in front of Essie and gently let down her veil over her face, and a black-garbed man I assumed was the rabbi invoked a blessing. I found I was standing next to Tali, the bridesmaid, who looked very sweet in a long lilac gown. "You know what it means?" she asked excitedly. "It's called 'Bedecken' and he just said, 'O sister, be thou the mother of thousands of tens thousands' like it was wished Rebecca in the Bible."

"I'll just bet she will be," I said under my breath. Tali moved toward Essie, and then I saw Adi's mother, Yael, and another woman, who I assumed was standing in for Essie's dead mother, carrying lighted candles and escorting the bride to the wedding canopy which was set up on the lawn. The four poles, decorated with roses, were being held by four kibbutznik friends of Adi's who looked virile enough to have won the War of Independence on their own.

I suddenly had a violent aversion to Israeli men, but I didn't really like anyone much, including myself, that day.

The candles were also new to me, survivor of dozens of Jewish weddings in London. They seemed pagan, but I looked up the explanation when I got home. The candles are associated with the thunder and lightning at the revelation on Mount Sinai, comparing the earthly ties of the human pair with the eternal bonding of Israel to God.

Adi had already been led to the chuppah by the two fathers and stood facing east toward Jerusalem. The rabbi was chanting as Essie came to join him, Tali holding on to the train of her gown for dear life. It was a simple wedding gown, modest, but in a lustrous satin that made it look very opulent and magnificent. My eyes were rooted to the pearl, which really did resemble a teardrop, an illusion aided by the real tears in my eyes that I hoped nobody would notice. Essie encircled the groom seven times and then stood next to him.

The rest of the ceremony was what I was used to, from the blessings over the wine, the betrothal blessing, and so on. Adi placed a ring on the forefinger of Essie's right hand and recited the marriage vow: *Harei at mekuddeshet li be-taba'at zo ke-dat Moshe v'Yisrael,* which even with my limited Hebrew, I knew meant: "Behold you are consecrated unto me by this ring, according to the Law of Moses and Israel." Soon after, I heard the shattering of the wineglass under Adi's foot, in memory of the destruction of the Temple in Jerusalem, and as it shattered, I knew that all my hopes and dreams of the future were crushed along with it.

I never really believed the saying that time heals, but now I have to admit there's some truth in it. I went back home determined to put Essie out of my mind completely, and eventually I managed it to the point where weeks would go by without my giving her a thought. Then I would read something about Israel in the paper or see a news item on television, and the dull ache would begin again.

But it didn't last long and London has many pleasures to offer of which I took full advantage.

Occasionally I would meet Ruth somewhere, but it was always by chance until she sent me an invitation to an exhibition of her paintings, about two years after our trip to Israel. She worked in a graphic design studio, but her true love was oil painting and she was a serious, talented artist. I had worked overtime at Reuters, so I arrived late to the opening. I was happy to see that a lot of paintings bore red "Sold" stickers on them. Ruth told me that a few art critics from the important papers had turned up and had spoken warmly to her, so she hoped for some good reviews. Most of the paintings were still lifes, a few were abstracts I really liked. There was one portrait. As I gravitated toward it, even from a distance, I could see it was of Essie. It must have been painted years ago when she lived with Ruth in London. In it, she sat with a notebook in her lap, a pen resting pensively against her chin, her lovely eyes full of wonder, the way I remembered her at twenty.

A giant lump had risen in my throat, and I knew I had to have the portrait at any price, even though I would never get Essie out of my system if I saw her face every day on my wall. I looked at the catalog and saw that it was marked: "Not for sale." I felt a mixture of sadness and relief. At least no stranger would possess it.

As the last of the viewers left, Ruth came over with a glass of champagne for me, sat down, and kicked off her elegant shoes.

"My feet are killing me. Thank heavens it's over."

"It's a great show, Ruth. I'm very impressed."

"Thanks. I've sold a lot of work and it's going to be on for two weeks. I didn't expect to sell the white lilac piece with the price tag I put on it, but I did. Actually I wanted to keep it, so I intentionally priced it exorbitantly, but someone liked it enough to pay it—and it wasn't even my mother." She laughed.

"The, er, portrait"—I tried to keep my voice casual—"you marked that one 'not for sale.'"

She looked at me shrewdly. "You realize it's Essie?"

I nodded. "The brushwork is excellent. I'd really like to buy it, Ruth."

She smiled. "The brushwork is lousy, as a matter of fact. It's one of my early pieces, but I wanted variety so I included the portrait. No, it's not for sale." She hesitated. "I miss Essie, too, Max. I always will. I'll never have another friend like her. She added color to everything, lit up the room in radiance; she took pleasure in life that I've never found with anyone else."

I nodded. "Let's go for supper," I said impetuously. "We have to celebrate your success."

We went to one of my haunts in Soho called The Omonia. It was a little Greek restaurant where the food was delicious, the music enchanting, and the clientele bohemian. Because it was so late, there were few diners left. Ruth and I caught up on each other's lives. Suddenly Ruth changed the subject.

"Max, you haven't had anyone special in your life since Essie?"

"Don't believe in it," I joked. "You know what they say, 'Why make one woman miserable when you can make so many happy'? But I haven't actually lived like a monk, if that's what you mean. What about you?"

"There was someone actually. We had a relationship for seven months. I really loved him, but"—her lips trembled—"he met someone else. An old story."

I squeezed her hand. It felt surprisingly good. "Maybe we can console each other," I was amazed to hear myself say.

"Maybe we can," she agreed.

And so it was I began to see a lot of Ruth. She wasn't Essie. She was a mature, experienced woman, and in addition to finding her desirable and attractive, I genuinely liked her. My mother also liked her, which was usually enough to turn me off a girl for good, but this time, for some reason, it didn't.

I was feeling very pleased with myself one evening, having just been appointed London bureau chief for Reuters. At my age it was a great feather in my cap. Ruth had made dinner for me in her flat to celebrate, and we were mellowed by the bottle of wine we'd just drunk, when she suddenly said:

"Max, would you like to move in with me?"

"What?"

"We spend so much time together, it seems silly to keep two places going."

"You mean, two can eat as cheaply as one?" I kidded, my mind unable to deal with it seriously.

"Something like that."

"What about your reputation?"

"What about it? If I don't care, why should you?"

But suddenly I did care; in fact, I felt very protective. I stopped the joking.

"Do you love me, Ruth?"

"I always have. But you never noticed me because of Essie."

"I'm noticing you now. I think I want to marry you."

"No, Max. I'd always be second best for you. My way is better."

I took her in my arms. "You're first and you're the only woman on my mind, I promise you."

"You don't have to marry me, Max. I'm not a virgin, you know."

"I don't care about that. Neither am I. But the future, that's something else."

"Have you really forgotten Essie?"

I couldn't lie to her. "Forgotten, no, gotten over, yes. I haven't seen or heard from her since her wedding. She may even have a child by now."

"She hasn't, surprisingly. She's having trouble conceiving."

I tried not to be glad or make a sarcastic remark that maybe her strong Israeli wasn't as virile as he looked. Then I felt disgusted with myself.

"Ruth, Essie is my past. I would like you to be my future. Will you marry me?"

She dissolved into tears, but assured me they were tears of happiness. I spent a long and most enjoyable time consoling her.

16

*R*uth and I were married in July 1958. I would have liked it to be just family, and Ruth was agreeable, but my mother had waited thirty-two years for this event so we did it her way—the family plus three hundred guests at London's fashionable Marble Arch synagogue, with a champagne reception afterward. The main reason, if I'm honest, I didn't want guests was that I didn't want Ruth to invite Essie and Adi. I really did want to forget her. Fortunately, they didn't come; maybe they couldn't afford the trip. I deliberately did not read the letter Essie wrote us, and I didn't ask which, of the hundreds of gifts we received, came from her.

We went for a honeymoon to Italy, and I was very happy. We saw Rome and Florence, Venice and Capri; it was a tender, loving time. Ruth filled the empty place that I had lived in for so many years, and I believed I was cured of Essie completely. When we returned to London, the portrait of her that Ruth had painted had disappeared and I asked no questions. I think I was glad that it had been replaced by a scene of London in a fog. I wasn't particularly impressed with that painting, but it had no power to hurt me.

We enjoyed our life together. We both earned good salaries, and I was making extra money as a freelancer for some prestigious American papers. Ruth participated in quite a few group shows and her work was commanding attention in the right places. We had bought a home in Richmond, with a view of the Thames. Our friends were an unlikely combination of artists and affluent people. It was a good marriage in every way. We were very engaged with each other, and we were both happy. It seemed natural that we should have a family, and fortune smiled on us in that endeavor, too. When we decided the time was right, Ruth conceived, had a trouble-free pregnancy, and delivered a healthy son. Jeremy looked remarkably like me and we adored him. Simon followed two years later and Tiffany—a miniature of Ruth—three years after that. We decided we had the perfect family and the perfect life.

I knew that Ruth and Essie continued to correspond, but she never showed me the letters, and if I took the mail inside and saw Essie's distinctive handwriting on an envelope, even though it was addressed to both of us, I never opened it. Ruth had started a stamp album for Jeremy, and when I saw the Israel section, I knew that letters must come quite frequently. Sometimes Ruth would make a tentative remark like: "It's such a pity that Essie has never managed to have a child," but the sentence would remain hanging in the air. I never found an adequate response and I was determined never to cause my wife pain by showing, even by an inflection of my voice, that Essie meant more to me than other women from my past.

But of course she did. I hadn't seen her for nine years, but the memory of her was always there just below the surface. There were places we had been together in London that I still avoided and, almost a decade later, I could not take my children to Hyde Park and Kensington Gardens. For me it was haunted.

My work also never let me entirely escape from the memory of Essie, because the newspapers were always full of headlines about Israel, and the two for me were indivisible. When the war broke out in

1967, I found myself sick with worry. It was Israel I talked about, but it was of Essie I was thinking. When I read the headlines that came through on ticker tape in our office: "Mirages Destroy Six Syrian MIGs" and "Jordan Shells Jerusalem," I had to crush an impulse to rush to Israel. Finally, rehearsing the words over and over before I could finally speak them, I managed to ask Ruth casually: "Where are Essie and Adi now?"

"Adi of course is in the army, but they are both still on the kibbutz. Do you think they'll be all right?" she asked anxiously.

We didn't know then that the war would be over in six days. Syria was sending out its own newspaper reports claiming that Israel had lost five Mirage jets and that seventy Israelis were killed along the border; and Amman Radio also dispensed its own propaganda. We weren't sure what to believe until we knew for sure that the Egyptians had been driven back to Sinai and Gaza and that finally the Old City of Jerusalem had fallen and was back in Israeli hands.

Like all Jews, even nonpracticing ones like us, it was a time of great euphoria, and we all celebrated as though the victory had personally been ours. Israel was suddenly the "good guy" in the eyes of the world, and Ruth suggested we should go there for our next holiday instead of Majorca as we had planned. But I couldn't do it; it would be unthinkable to be in Israel and not see Essie—and I wasn't that much of a masochist that I wanted the pain all over again. Of course, there was always the possibility that seeing her after so many years would finally end it, because I was truly happy with Ruth and our wonderful kids. It might be that my feelings for her were only a memory and I just hadn't realized it. Nevertheless, I wasn't willing to take the chance.

"It would be a pity to take the kids to Israel when they're so young," I said evasively. "It won't mean anything to them and they won't remember it."

"Jeremy's six," Ruth reminded me. "He never forgets anything."

"Still . . ."

She looked at me shrewdly. "Does it still hurt so much?"

I could have won an Academy Award for my acting. "What?" I asked, looking genuinely perplexed.

"Max, one day we have to talk about it. You're still in love with Essie, aren't you? It's painful for me, Max. I'm not asking you to forget her altogether . . ."

"Don't be ridiculous," I said crossly. "My not wanting to go to Israel just now has nothing to do

with Essie, if that's what you're thinking. I just don't
fancy schlepping three kids all over Israel. In
Majorca, we'll all lie in the sun on the beach and
relax. You can't relax in Israel—it's too raw; there's
always too much happening."

"We could lie on the beach in Eilat," she suggested. Ruth had no way of knowing I had spent a
holiday there with Essie, or that it was there I finally
knew I had lost her. For one moment I was unable
to prevent the naked look of loss before I turned my
back and got busy with some papers. But she had
seen it. Her eyes filled with tears.

"Even now?" she whispered.

I took her in my arms. "I love you, Ruth—you're
my life," I reassured her. And it was true. Ruth and
the children were my reality; I couldn't imagine life
without them. Essie was a wraith, a haunting melody
that I could never completely silence. Ruth and I
made love then, with great tenderness. I think she
was convinced, and I tried so hard to convince
myself.

I really did put Essie completely out of my mind over the next few years. Her letters continued to come—not very often—but wisely Ruth kept her own counsel and never discussed their contents with me. Sometimes I would have liked to know if she'd had children, but was afraid that even such a simple question would open up a Pandora's box for Ruth. Normally she was a secure and self-confident woman, and not at all jealous. We often ran into girls I had known quite well, and we could tease each other about them. But Essie was not in the same category.

The kids had a week's school holiday, but since it was a hectic time for me at work, Ruth and her girlfriend—who also had three children—rented a house in Bournemouth and went off to enjoy themselves, leaving the husbands behind.

As far as I knew, Essie's letters only came about four times a year, but on the second day of Ruth's vacation, there in the mailbox was the familiar rounded writing on the blue envelope, and the Israeli stamp.

Fate can be cruel and perhaps generous at the same time. As hard as I tried to forget her, and as good as my life was—and it was very good—I was fated always to long for Essie. I just couldn't shake it. There are people in your life you simply never forget, as if they had imprinted themselves on your soul. We can love more than one person in our lives. One person can remain alive within us even as we are actively engaged with someone else. Essie left her mark on me and it could never be erased. I suffered for that love, but I wouldn't have missed experiencing it for the world.

I took her letter out of the mailbox gingerly, as though it might explode. It was, as usual, addressed to both of us, but in twelve years I had not opened nor read one of the letters. I put it on the mantel with a few other letters for Ruth, but all through dinner my eyes returned to it like a magnet. Something about it was different. I took it down and examined it again. Of course—the postmark. I went and got Jeremy's stamp album; every Israeli stamp was cancelled with the name Ayalon, the area of the kibbutz. This one said Jerusalem.

"It doesn't mean anything," I told myself. "She could have been there for the day, or a holiday. It's only a forty-minute bus ride."

I put it back and turned on the TV. I watched some program about recovering alcoholics, and felt like one myself as my eyes kept returning to the envelope, much as I imagine an AA member would be hypnotized by a bottle.

Finally, my curiosity overcame me. Although my name was also on the envelope, somehow I could not tear it open. It would mean another discussion with Ruth, more need for reassurance, for explanations. I turned the gas up under the kettle until there was a fierce blast of steam and, feeling like a criminal, I steamed it open.

Dear Ruth and Max,

I feel very guilty about not having written in so long. The photos of the children that you sent are wonderful—how tall Jeremy and Simon are, and how very feminine is Tiffany. You are lucky to have such treasures. You will see that I have a new address. Yes, I'm living again in my beloved Jerusalem. It is a bittersweet experience, because I am here on my own. Adi and I were divorced a few months ago. There is no simple way to explain what happened, because it wasn't the result of any one thing. I suppose if we'd had children, perhaps we would have stayed together for their sake, but that miracle never happened. I had four miscarriages over the years and I am resigned to the fact that I will never have children of my own. I hope Adi will remarry—I'm sure he will—and that he'll have a family and the kind of wife I tried to be, but never quite managed.

It was an amicable divorce, if that's the right word, which is why it was so quick. We still have a lot of affection for each other. Receiving the get, *the bill of divorcement, was quite traumatic. In the ceremony you cup your hands and the paper the* get *is written on floats between them. It felt so strange.*

Religion was never the problem; it gave my life an extra dimension and I won't discard it now— although I no longer cover my hair as I did before. I think the kibbutz itself was the problem; I had been stifled by it for the past few years and Adi could never leave it nor would I expect him to do so.

It was such a closed community, the same faces, the same routines, day after day, year after year, and the singular focus on family. Though that sense of connectedness around a belief and a purpose meant so much to me when I was younger, little by little I found myself feeling alien. I tried to fit in, but I didn't and grew restless. More and more I began to escape to Jerusalem to meet with other writers and poets. I never lost my need to create, to write, but I lacked stimulation and people to talk to. When I made my decision to leave after ten years I hardly needed to tell Adi; he already knew. In a way I think it was a relief for him.

I'm sorry this is such a maudlin letter. I am not so unhappy because my love affair with Jerusalem is passionate and ongoing, and now I am here, I hope, forever. It's like coming home.

I've always treasured sharing my poems with you, Ruth, just as I so treasure the sketches and paintings you send me. This one was written before I had quite come to terms with my situation, so don't let it depress you too much.

My love to Max and the children.

Affectionately,
Essie

The poem was on a separate page. I read it several times and then I did something I hadn't done since I was a kid: I put my head down on my arms and cried.

Jerusalem Summer

Ramat Rachel in summer haze
Muted. Golden yellow canvas striped
With shadows of midnight blue.
Pine trees sighing in the afternoon
Whisper secrets that I understand.
Below lies Bethlehem
Breathless and pregnant
With silent secrets of its own.
Somewhere down there a tomb
Holds Rachel of the sorrows,
Rachel weeping for her children
While candles burn and tourists
Stand curious, embarrassed,
Trying to remember if it were she
or sister Leah whom Jacob loved,
But I am on the hill
Above Rachel and her sadness . . .
There is enough of my own
To burden this golden day.
Halfway journeyed through life
(Perhaps much more than half?)
Weighed down by too many dreams
Never to be fulfilled;
Too many attempts at love

Left unconsummated.
Only in distance lies consolation . . .
The dreams still in the future
May yet have a chance.
So I stand on a hill
In Jerusalem's breathless summer
And I gaze to the distance—
Hardly noticing the tears.

I could hardly believe Jeremy was already old enough to be bar mitzvahed. It was already 1973, where was the time going? Still, we were all excited, particularly the grandparents. We planned a big party after the service and Ruth was indulging in an orgy of shopping: new suits for the boys, dresses for her and Tiffany at a price that would have paid the national debt. But for once I didn't quibble.

But two weeks before the bar mitzvah the Yom Kippur War broke out, and we were all shaken. Israel again was attacked. Israel again at war. Screaming headlines: "Tanks Battle as Syrians Penetrate Golan Line"; "Egyptians Cross Canal"; "Bitter Battles Raging."

Once I would have said it was not our war, we were citizens of Britain, but—even if we didn't keep two sets of dishes—we were Jews and Israel had become embedded in our conscience. We could not turn our backs and go on with our lives while she struggled for survival. There was not a lot we could do except show some kind of solidarity and, of course, cancel the big party we had planned. Jeremy was mature enough to understand; we made it up to him in other ways, with an extravagant chemistry set that could have blown us into the next world if he'd misused it. This time I didn't keep silent about my concern for Essie, which Ruth shared and felt as deeply as I did.

"She could come back to London," Ruth insisted.

"Could you imagine Essie leaving now?" I asked.

Her letters filtered through and I began to read them openly. I think Ruth believed I was long past any kind of romantic entanglement. And I wasn't thinking of Essie at this point in any way except as one would of a dear friend living in one of the most dangerous cities in the world.

The letters were remarkably calm and very optimistic. She referred to the war, but only in the context of her daily life. She wrote about her work; she was a copywriter again, with a large Jerusalem news agency, writing text for newpapers in both Hebrew and English.

I tried to look for clues about another man in her life, although truthfully the possibility no longer worried me. But if there was, she didn't mention him. She did write about a novel she was working on, called *In a Green Pasture,* about new immigrants coming to Israel without knowing exactly why. Her theory was that this migration was part of "The Ingathering of the Exiles," as predicted in the Bible when Jews were brought from the four corners of the earth and planted within its borders. It was a very spiritual idea and, I think, explained her own unlikely settlement in Israel.

Eventually the war ended, and the frightening headlines I'd been dealing with were replaced by more moderate ones like: "Accord on Disengagement Today: Elazar and Gamasy to Sign Document at Km. 101."

We were able to forget about Israel and get on with our lives. London was changing; in some ways, it was becoming more sophisticated, but I missed the gracious way of life which seemed to have disappeared forever. It was becoming strident, and I couldn't bear to watch the increasing numbers of homeless that slept in the doorways of the glittering stores in the affluent West End. Whenever we went to the theater, there was always the chill of seeing these pathetic souls when we came out.

Living in Richmond, we were cushioned from much of the darker side of life. It was a good life, but the contrast was unsettling. Selfishly, perhaps, we ignored the less fortunate when we didn't come face to face with them, giving generous amounts of charity to salve our conscience. Ruth often had one-woman shows at one of the many local galleries; the kids had loads of friends, we had a favorite pub where, true to stereotype, we even played darts. Life was smooth and trouble-free and we felt that fortune was smiling on us.

It was while reading one of the Sunday papers that Ruth gave a cry of delight. "I don't believe it. How wonderful. Come and look at this!"

It was just a small paragraph on the literary page announcing that Essie's book had been awarded the Forsythe Prize: a large sum of money, plus publication by Greenfield and Richman, a leading British publishing house. Neither the donors nor the publishers had any Jewish or Israeli connection, so it was indeed a tribute to the literary merit of her novel, for surely the subject she had chosen would have been more of a liability than an asset. Israel was no longer the world's darling, as it had been after the Six-Day War or the Entebbe mission to Uganda.

Israel-bashing had again become a popular pastime in the world press. Ruth was excited for her friend, and I, too, was thrilled. I had never wanted to believe that the talent I had sensed so many years ago had been completely extinguished by what seemed to me the wrong choices she had made in her life.

It was a great surprise that Essie, despite what I considered handicaps she had voluntarily taken on herself, had somehow managed to devote herself to her writing. Still, I always knew there was so much to Essie. I was so proud she had won the Forsythe Prize. Perhaps some British snobbery was seeping in, or perhaps her winning a British prize brought her closer to me in some way.

Ruth sent her a large basket of exotic flowers through Interflora and wrote both our names on the card. Apart from resolving to read the novel as soon as it came out, I was content to leave it at that.

But Essie always had a way of moving in and out of my life in unexpected ways. When I first met her, we used to dance to the melody, "You Keep Coming Back Like a Song." And that's how it felt. Essie was a song that played over and over again in my heart. We'd danced in her little attic room after we'd been to the theater. Radio Luxembourg used to play it late at night before their closing refrain of "Goodnight Sweetheart," which was always my cue to go home. Never once did she let me stay after midnight. My colleagues and friends would today hoot with laughter if they heard me described as sentimental, but the truth is I never heard that song without remembering Essie.

Anyway, she did keep coming back, for it was only a few weeks after reading about her award that a very fancy envelope arrived, addressed to me and Ruth. It came on a Saturday morning while Ruth had taken Tiffany to her ballet class, so I opened it automatically, assuming it was either an invitation to a wedding or a bar mitzvah. But, in gold embossed lettering on the same thick parchment as the envelope, it read:

Greenfield and Richman, Publishers
have much pleasure in inviting you to a Cocktail Party
to congratulate Esther Goodman on winning
the Forsythe Prize for her novel
In a Green Pasture
The author will be arriving from Israel for the occasion.
The party will be held at the
Savoy Hotel on Thursday, 8 June 1976
Cocktails at 6.30 P.M.
R.S.V.P. 25 May

A number of conflicting emotions hit me all at once, as they always did where Essie was concerned. I felt a wave of pleasure that she had reverted to her maiden name; somehow this hadn't registered when Ruth first showed me the announcement in the paper. Then I felt disgusted with myself: What sort of a bastard, happily married himself, would rejoice in the fact of another's failed marriage?

I felt a mixture of both pleasure and dread at the prospect of seeing her again. Essie would be forty-two now. What if she were completely different? An image of Golda Meir drifted to my mind, and I laughed at myself.

I suddenly realized how much I was thinking about Essie, and it distressed me; I seriously thought I was over her. But she could never be nothing to me—my Essie, my first love. Perhaps the truism that you never get over the first love of your life was true for me.

I read the invitation again. I hated cocktail parties, although we went to our fair share of them. I also felt a sense of panic that Ruth would be surreptitiously watching me, monitoring my every reaction to seeing Essie again after so many years.

My sense of the whole thing was not good, and I could feel disaster coming as surely as watching a child walk into oncoming traffic. Not unexpectedly, a couple of hours later, Ruth and I had a major argument, which was rare between us. I felt horrible.

I left the invitation on the hall table in the middle of a stack of letters, several of which I'd opened. I hoped it would look casual—of no importance— which is why I'd stuck the invitation in the middle, although I'd really agonized over it for about ten minutes. It was ridiculous, really. Whenever anything to do with Essie came up, I stopped being a mature man about to celebrate his fiftieth birthday—and rather suave, my mirror assured me—and instead my behavior became decidedly adolescent. I also decided not to mention it unless Ruth did, and then only in an offhand way.

I didn't have to wait long. Within a few minutes of hearing the front door bang, Ruth came into my study where I was distractedly reading a book. I must have been reading the same page thirty-seven times.

"Did you see the invitation?"

I could hardly deny it, considering I'd opened it.

"Oh yes," I said vaguely. "Very nice . . ."

"It's wonderful," Ruth enthused. "I think we should invite Essie to stay with us. After all, we've got plenty of room."

"No, that's not a good idea at all," I said hastily.

"She hasn't been to London for years; she should be in the West End where all the action is—you know, publishers, agents, and so on . . ." I trailed off.

"Nonsense. She'd love to get to know our children. We could make our own little party for her and take her around a bit."

"She wouldn't eat our food," I said desperately. "We're not kosher."

"Oh, that's easy. I'll serve vegetarian and there are dozens of kosher caterers I could use if we gave her a party."

"Ruth, no!" I said loudly. "We'll go to her party at the Savoy, and you can take her out every day if you want to while I'm busy at work. But I don't want her to stay here."

"I want to talk about this, Max."

"Well, I don't."

"She's my friend, Max, the best one I ever had."

"So, she'll still be your friend."

"You don't trust yourself around her, do you?"

"Let's drop it, shall we? I'm glad her book's a success, that you'll see her again, et cetera, et cetera. But it's my house, too, and I don't want her staying here."

"Why not?"

I groaned. "Ruth, leave it be. I'm not still in love

with her if that's what you're thinking; in fact, I haven't thought of her in years. If you're happy she's coming, that's fine with me, too, but I'm not letting her disrupt our lives."

Ruth spoke deliberately and painfully. "I don't understand, Max. We have guests all the time. You enjoy them; you never complain they are disrupting our lives. Why is it different with Essie, if you say you're no longer in love with her?"

"It just is. I can't explain it." That at least was true.

Ruth finally seemed to accept it, but it cast a blight on our weekend. For the first time we pursued separate activities and our conversation at mealtimes was stilted and cold—and Essie hadn't even arrived in England yet.

19

We didn't discuss Essie's forthcoming visit in the next few weeks, but it always hung somewhere in the air between us. I knew Ruth resented the fact that she couldn't call her in Jerusalem and extend an open invitation to stay with us. Ruth was a warm, generous woman and I had cast a pall on her happiness at the prospect of spending time with one of her oldest and dearest friends. I might have relented if I'd felt that Essie's trip would be financially difficult for her, but the prize she had won was substantial, and I was sure that all the expenses would be taken care of by her publisher, in any case. Apart from the cocktail party, they would probably get good mileage out of her: an interview on the BBC, some TV guest programs, signing copies at Foyle's or some other big bookstore, probably even publicity trips to the provinces. Greenfield and Richman knew how to milk every drop of publicity value from their authors, and my feeling was that Essie would be kept very busy. Coming from Jerusalem would add an exotic touch, too—this was before the time Israeli tourists overran London on frantic shopping sprees.

I couldn't picture Essie in that context, though. She wasn't really a tourist. London had once been home to her. Shopping sprees were just not the sort of thing she did.

With the impending arrival of Essie, a coldness was growing between Ruth and myself. We were scrupulously polite to each other, but the affectionate bantering was gone. Even though I was cowardly on the subject of Essie, I decided that not talking about the problem was even worse.

A week before the cocktail party I called Ruth from work and asked her to meet me in the West End for dinner.

"What's the occasion?" she asked innocently.

"Does there have to be an occasion? Maybe I just want to be seen dining out with a pretty woman?"

"What about the children?"

"Jeremy's sixteen, he can look after Tiffany and Simon. He even knows how to cook. They'll be fine."

"I suppose so," she said uncertainly, and a little unenthusiastically.

Now I was becoming a bit irritable and regretted the whole idea, but we fixed a time and place and met for dinner. It was a restaurant we both liked and when Ruth arrived I felt my anger melt away. I reached for her hand across the table.

"I want to apologize."

"For what?"

"Spoiling Essie's visit for you."

She didn't answer, but her eyes moistened.

"Look honey, she's just a memory for me, you understand? You are my reality. And I want to keep it that way. I'll be happy to see her in a crowded room, give her my congratulations, and then get back to my real life, which is you and the children."

"I think what you're really saying is she still has the power to evoke strong feelings in you and you don't trust yourself to be with her."

"It's not like that at all."

"Then what is it like? You never answer me."

"I don't know how to answer you. She once meant a lot to me, but we were never lovers. . . ."

"I understand."

"I did want to marry her, but didn't because she turned me down. She wanted me to come to Israel and live as an Orthodox Jew. I think if I'd been insane enough to live in Israel, she might have said yes. But you see, I couldn't have loved her all that much because I never considered moving to Israel, and I certainly never could become religious the way she wanted me to. So in a way I rejected her as well."

I waited for Ruth to interrupt, but she kept silent, although she still held on to my hand.

"But you always were so special to me, Ruth. You still are."

"I was never sure why."

"After all these years, you still have to ask? I fell in love with you and you made me happy. You gave me a home, a life I felt happy in. With Essie, I may have been wandering the universe. If Essie stayed with us, it could cause complications. You'd be suspicious of all our conversations and overly sensitive to all kinds of things. That could threaten both the stability of our marriage, and even make you jealous of your friend. What would be the point?"

"I suppose you're right. I just don't want Essie to feel I'm shortchanging her."

"She'll never think that. You're the most generous friend in the world. I want you to spend as much time with her as you wish—every day if you want—

but I think it's better if I stay in the background. She'll understand."

She nodded. We seemed to have cleared the air for the moment, and we finally got around to ordering dinner. But life never let me get off so easily . . . never where Essie was concerned!

The cocktail party was much as I expected it to be—frightful. We arrived about halfway through, when the champagne cocktails had already freely circulated, loosening everyone's lips. It had reached the stage where husbands and wives were surreptitiously trying to lose each other in order to test out other possibilities. Everyone referred to each other as "darling," even when they were obviously strangers. The noise from the milling reviewers and publishing staff and media people and hangers-on was deafening. No one looked even remotely like they could be a friend to Essie; I guess Ruth was the only one from our early days who had kept in touch.

I was searching with my eyes among the many women for someone who just might be Essie. I found her just as Ruth said, "There she is!" She was standing quite apart, near the window, looking unusually lost. Fortunately, she bore no resemblance to Golda Meir! If I had conjured what I wanted her to look like, that's how she looked. Her hair was silver and hung to her shoulders in a shimmering curtain. She wore a simple black dress and a string of pearls. Among all the bejeweled, elegantly coiffed women, she was like an oasis in the desert, and even seemed to have an aura of purity surrounding her. In spite of myself, I whispered, "My God!" Ruth had already rushed to her side.

It is a well-known superstition that if the gods want to punish you, they grant you your wish. That's how I felt watching Essie at an anonymous distance; it was painful to see her, much as I longed for the opportunity. Among the crowd of pseudo-intellectuals moving about in the elegant room, she stood apart in a little pool of silence—elegant, dignified, and heartbreakingly desirable.

Everything seemed to be moving in slow motion. I saw Ruth embrace Essie, and watched as Essie's lost look transformed into delight. I was only a few feet away, but it felt as though it took forever to cross the short expanse of burgundy carpet to join them. I didn't know what kind of impression to arrange on my face. I felt as though I'd been kicked in the stomach, and all I could muster was an absurdly false grin as I approached her.

She kissed me on the cheek as affectionately and naturally as if I were her brother, and I didn't know whether to be relieved or disappointed. I felt sad. It was clear the earth hadn't moved for her at seeing me again. As for me, her powerful, moving presence had overtaken me, as always; shock waves were registering on my internal Richter scale.

She was holding both of Ruth's hands and listening delightedly to whatever Ruth was saying. I stood there, contributing nothing, but nodding and smiling at the appropriate times.

I heard them making plans for lunch the next day and for Essie to meet the children. They were still exchanging plans for the next two weeks when a distinguished-looking gentleman, who turned out to be one of the publishers—either Greenfield or Richman—came over and took Essie gently by the elbow, obviously wanting to introduce her to some new arrivals. She gave us a remorseful smile as she went off with him.

"Well, that's that," I said with some relief to Ruth, nudging her toward the door. But of course it wasn't.

For the next week I managed to bury myself in my
work, coming home later than usual. My intuition of
the busy schedule that Essie would have to follow
proved correct, and her publishers filled her diary
with commitments. Nevertheless, she spent part of
every day with Ruth, even if it was only a hurried
lunch in a coffee shop. Each evening Ruth would
prattle on happily about where they'd been
together, and I would nod and smile as though
everything were fine. In another week she'd be
gone, and no major traumas had taken place. The
only time I nearly blew my cool was when Ruth told
me of her plan to subject Essie to a makeover.

"I thought I'd book Essie for a full day at one of
the major cosmetic houses for a makeover."

"A what?"

"Well, they pamper you very extravagantly. You
have a facial and a manicure and a massage. They'll
give her a new hairdo and a new color. I mean it's
ridiculous for her to be gray at forty-five. She'd be
stunning, say, as a redhead."

In my mind, it was like letting Max Factor loose
on the Mona Lisa. My stomach tightened. "It's not a
good idea, Ruth."

"Why not? I'd love it."

"Yes, but you're different. Besides, her hair is very

pretty as it is. It's not really gray; it's more like silver."

For once, Ruth didn't argue. "Maybe you're right," she said casually. I felt my luck was changing, at last.

But just in case I got too comfortable, the very next day fate knocked me for a loop. I had just stepped into the elevator on my way up to my office in Fleet Street, when Essie stepped in just after me. I thought I was hallucinating.

"Max . . . oh . . . what a coincidence." I could see she, too, was taken aback. "It was so good seeing you the other night . . ." she said, as she pulled back that familiar slip of hair that had loosened from the rest. Even with her new hairdo, she still couldn't control that errant lock. She was still so Essie, so poised, but so vulnerable.

"What are you doing here?" I interrupted her. I was so shocked to see her. Somehow I'd convinced myself I would never come this close to her again, despite her being in London.

"*Australian Women's Weekly,* on the third floor," she said quickly, trying to regain her composure. "They want to interview me. You know, local girl makes good."

"And haven't you? We're so proud," I said, as though I were her father. As she began to walk away

I felt an overwhelming sense of loss all over again. I waited a second and suddenly I yelled, "Essie, wait. Will you come up and visit me in my office afterward?" The invitation slipped from my lips before I realized it.

She looked a little confused, but there was no hesitation in her answer: "Okay, Max." She smiled and I could feel her really looking at me, as if recognizing someone who had been important to her. "It's been so long, hasn't it?"

"Yes," I answered, my heart pounding inside my chest.

$\mathcal{I}$t was more than an hour before she came up to my office, and I'd been pacing the floor like an expectant father, worried that she wasn't coming and terrified that she was. I couldn't help but become possessed of the memory of our first meeting here in this very office. How could a life be like this, I wondered? How could one want something so badly and not get it? I knew all the answers, rationally, but there was no emotional logic to it at all.

In some sense I couldn't even say what made me fall so in love with Essie. Was it some unexpressed part of myself that I found in her? Her dynamic nature? I did love Ruth, yet she and Essie were night and day. Ruth was stable, settled, conventional, but had a lively intellect. Essie was a trailblazer, always moving about; she was her own person, singular in her sensibilities. Excitement always seemed to surround her. And yet there was something ineffable about her, some longing for life that moved me beyond words.

Since I was bureau chief now, aspects of the office had become somewhat grander, but little else had changed. I had to admit I still wanted to impress Essie. We were both a lot older and each, in our own way, had "made" it: I as a journalist and she as an author. Yet everything seemed curiously the same.

London was drifting toward twilight as the shadows lengthened and the traffic noises seemed muted. The ghost of twenty-year-old Essie filled the room even while I was waiting for her flesh and blood successor to arrive.

When she did arrive, it was not breathlessly as it had been the first time. She knocked and stood poised on the threshold, waiting to be invited in. She'd become a stunningly beautiful woman. She'd always been attractive, but only in the pretty way that most young girls are. Now she looked to me as a work of art that grows more profound with time. Essie's beauty had always been located in her complexity, and as a mature woman she was absolutely radiant. She was wearing, as she always did, a simple dress, but of a lovely coral linen. Perhaps she had enough money now to buy things that suited her expressive taste. As I gazed at her, I suddenly noticed that she was wearing the single pearl teardrop I had given her on her wedding day. I nearly gasped. Did she think of me whenever she wore it?

"Essie, please, please sit down." I'd been thinking about her so intently, I hadn't realized I'd forgotten to actually greet her.

"Are you sure I'm not interrupting your work, Max?"

"No, no, no, Essie. I got so distracted for a minute. . . . It's so good to see you here."

We both searched for something to say, and I wondered why I had asked her to come.

"How was your interview?" was all I could come up with.

"I think it went well, very well. In fact, I actually think I enjoyed it."

I hesitated to speak, but I couldn't avoid all that was on my mind. I was bursting to talk to her. I stood up from behind my desk and walked around to sit on its corner to be closer to her. I could practically feel her in my arms. "Do you remember, Essie? This is where we first met."

"Yes." She smiled, sadly, her mood changing from her earlier exuberance. "But somehow it doesn't seem so very long ago." Her look was both fragile and sure. It was one of the things about her I'd always been seduced by—her ability to sustain two conflicting emotions.

Suddenly, her entire demeanor lightened once again as she jumped out of her chair and grabbed something on my desk. For a moment, she was the young Essie again. "Look!" she cried. She was holding the statue of *The Thinker,* the same one with which she was so delighted the day we met. "You still have it. It's wonderful to find it here again. Do you think he's still thinking about the same thing?"

Again, her mood changed and she grew somber and then agitated as her eyes filled. "But this is ridiculous. Why am I getting so emotional about this? I made important decisions in my life, good and bad decisions both, and so did you. Our lives are different, separate. They have been for a very long time." She put the statue gently back on the desk, nudging it back to its exact spot.

I was shocked by her sudden outburst and responded with the same bluntness. "It doesn't matter; I've never stopped thinking about you."

"I know how you *think* you feel about me, maybe. But, Max, you don't know me anymore. Too much has happened in my life."

"A lot of things have happened to me, too, Essie. But it didn't change any of my feelings for you. I died a little bit when you went out of my life. Didn't I matter to you?"

"It wouldn't have worked," she answered, avoiding the real question.

"Why not? I loved you so much."

"Love?" she whispered, laughing quietly to herself. I was confused to see Essie respond that way. She was many things, but cynical? No. I was supposed to be the cynic. She believed in love. I was certain of it.

"Unfortunately, I learned, as many of us do, that love is a word that can be used to justify doing all kinds of hurtful things. Adi used it to justify his ownership of me, until I finally felt strangled by him and left."

For the first time she looked a little beaten down and worn out. I remembered the eager young girl looking for experience, desperate and excited to find the shape of her own identity. I knew that process wouldn't be easy, but it was part of the expansive spirit that drove her.

"I wouldn't have done that to you, Essie."

"You wouldn't have done it intentionally. Nor did Adi. He wanted me to be happy, but he also wanted to make me into a mirror-image of his mother and all the other kibbutz wives. I tried to fill that role. I thought that was what I wanted, too. It's not entirely his fault. I confused possession with love as well."

"Essie, I saw you as a free spirit. I would never have wanted you to conform to anything. When I watched you becoming religious I knew you would have to suppress so much of yourself—your spontaneity, for one thing."

She smiled. "Max, you don't understand. Becoming *dati*, becoming religious, was a liberation for me in spite of it all. It took something away but it gave me something, too. I was born a Jew, but when I was younger being Jewish was a burden for me; I had no idea what it meant. I tried to pretend I was exactly the same as my gentile friends; really like those who were lapsed Catholics. And then, when I came to Israel, it was like discovering a gift I'd always possessed but never knew I had."

I felt uncomfortable. Whether she knew it or not, she was describing my life. I never denied being Jewish to my colleagues, but I never talked about it either. I felt a kind of gratitude when my non-Jewish friends acclaimed my work, invited me to their homes. Their approval was necessary for my own self-esteem. I hurried to change the subject.

"But Adi was all wrong for you. He didn't under-stand your potential or your talent."

"I think it was more that I was wrong for him. He is a good man, and if we'd had children, I know he would have been a wonderful father."

She got up and stood at the window gazing down on Fleet Street, now a mass of black shapes inter-spersed with golden dots of light. At the end, the massive presence of St. Paul's loomed.

"We could have had it all. I don't care what you say, we would have been so good together."

"Max, I don't know what could have been. You meant so much to me—the world, in fact. I felt so close to you. But the decisions I made I had to make. What could I do? And we can never go back."

I longed to take her in my arms. I moved toward her, but she put her hands out in front of her in a helpless, vulnerable way. I waited.

"Max, please, don't. We'd only hurt someone we both love."

"Essie, my love, do you have any idea what I have gone through all these years?"

She brushed her lips gently against mine and before I could react, she quickly escaped through the door, closing it firmly behind her.

Essie had accused me of not really knowing her, and when I finally got around to reading her novel, I had to admit she was right. *In a Green Pasture* was not what I would have expected her to write. I suppose for me she was forever locked into a time warp: twenty years old, full of dreams, a naive girl taking her first steps into the world.

It was written by a woman who had endured a lot of pain in her life, but nevertheless had emerged not cynical but victorious. It was a celebration of life.

The title had meant nothing to me, but as I should have guessed, it was based on a biblical quotation—Ezek. 34:12–14:

> *As a shepherd seeketh out his flock on the day that he is among his sheep that are scattered, so will I seek*

out my sheep, and will deliver them out of all places
where they have been scattered in the cloudy and dark
day.

And I will bring them out from the peoples, and
gather them from the countries and will bring them to
their own land, and feed them upon the mountains
of Israel by the rivers, and in all the inhabited places
of the country. I will feed them in a good pasture and
upon the high mountains of Israel shall their fold be;
there shall they lie in a good fold, and in a fat pas-
ture shall they feed upon the mountains of Israel.

The novel was set mostly in an absorption center
for new immigrants in 1971, and the characters
were a class of beginning students in the Ulpan,
from widely diverse backgrounds, united only by the
fact that they were thrown together for six months
to learn Hebrew.

Two of the characters were particularly well drawn:
a woman called Lee from Reno, Nevada, who was the
illegitimate daughter of an alcoholic Jewish mother
and a Christian father who had abandoned them
when she was a small child, and a Spanish homo-
sexual named José, portrayed with great tenderness.
I felt sure he was based on someone she had known;
her insights were far too perceptive for him to have

been invented. There was also an Australian named Freda, whom I guessed had been based on her own life, but she was not nearly as colorful as some of the other characters.

It was not a novel with a "happy ever after" ending. Few of the six main characters got what they wanted out of life, yet some of them got what they needed, which was different.

Lee had been portrayed early in the novel as a vain and shallow woman, a product of a society without values. By the end she had learned a valuable lesson, that survival is in itself a mitzvah—a commandment and a kind of blessing. In the twenty-two years I had known Essie she had become a survivor, too: transplanted from her native soil to a country that was never free of tension and hardship. She also survived her deep disappointment in not having had children, and of a failed marriage. She had overcome everything to become a respected author, an independent and successful woman. She was more than a survivor, she was a victor.

Strangely enough, by comparison I felt I had lost. I had all the economic advantages, a prestigious job, a beautiful home, a charming wife and family. There was little money could buy that I hadn't acquired, and yet I was never really satisfied, I always felt something was missing. Essie inferred that I was going after the wrong things, but I felt that she was what was missing. There were times in my life when not being with her produced a sharp pain, and I got used to it over the years. Other times her absence was a dull ache, and then I didn't feel it at all. But she was always there.

I didn't go to the airport to say good-bye to Essie when she left London, although Ruth did. Instead I went and got smashed—something I hadn't done in years. I was ashamed of myself and told Ruth I'd been to a Buck's Night for a guy who was getting married. It sounded thin even to me because Ruth knew all my friends and no wedding invitation had materialized. Whatever she thought, she kept it to herself, and I was grateful. She kept the kids out of my way the next morning when I had a giant hangover. The horrendous noise that came crashing out of Jeremy's room early in the morning, which he called music, was terminated abruptly by Ruth's intervention just when I was trying to get up the strength to go in and turn it off. Ruth was gentle and solicitous to me, which made me feel like a giant louse, and consequently I reacted brusquely and impatiently. I am sure that when I finally got myself off to work, the whole family heaved a sigh of relief.

It is hard to pinpoint when things start to turn sour in a marriage, but I guess this was about the time when ours must have started to slide downhill. We didn't have arguments; to outsiders, we must still have looked a model family. The house continued to be an open one to all the kids' friends. Ruth and I pursued an active social life, although not always together. Saturday night was still our night for socializing as a couple. Usually we'd go out to dinner and to the theater in the West End with friends, and often we'd finish up at a fashionable nightclub and dance or enjoy the floor show. But weeknights changed. I didn't seem to have the energy or desire to keep up with Ruth and her bohemian friends, although not long ago I'd enjoyed them. I found them increasingly pretentious. Ruth was a serious artist, and I began to wonder why she wasted her time with them.

Other things began to irritate me as well. I'd always been proud of Ruth's beauty and the way she dressed and carried herself. But suddenly everything about her looked and felt wrong. I wasn't exactly happy with myself and all these bad feelings. Somewhere along the way everything in my life seemed to have been drained of its former pleasure.

The year 1982 was not, as Frank Sinatra would have it, a very good year. Maybe there don't seem to be many more good years when you've just turned fifty-six and are not feeling too good about yourself. Not that I looked much different—I still had all my hair, all my teeth, and I hadn't developed a paunch.

What I had developed was a giant dissatisfaction with my life. When you've reached the top, which I had, there doesn't seem anywhere else to go. The house felt empty, with both Jeremy and Simon away at university, Jeremy studying architecture and Simon messing around with a lot of esoteric languages like Chinese and Russian. He had no idea what he'd do with them—he spoke vaguely of the Foreign Office—and probably saw himself in some kind of James Bond role. Even Tiffany, who was seventeen, was supposedly studying for her A-levels, though seemingly majoring in boys. I remember thinking to myself somewhat poetically: *This is the winter of my discontent.*

Probably most of my discontent had to do with this particular period of my life. I wasn't getting a lot of joy from my kids, and Ruth accused me of being jealous of their youth. I probably was. Mostly I was jealous of the years ahead of them to fulfill all their dreams. Whatever dreams I'd started out with I had either lost along the way, or they had gone sour when I achieved them.

Although Ruth was only a few years younger, she had a lot more energy to fight the encroaching years; a holiday alone in Switzerland had turned out to be for a face-lift, and she came back sparkling. She still dressed too youthfully in overly bright colors, but I often heard her and Tiffany giggling together like sisters, rather than mother and daughter, and I felt excluded. However, now and again, I would look at her from behind and see the telltale wrinkled elbows that betrayed the age that her face denied. Then I would feel protective toward her and concerned about the relentless battle she waged against middle age, and which she could never win.

I continued to hear of Essie, although I'd had no direct contact with her since her award trip to London. She'd written two more books, both successful, but this time they were published in America. She wrote in English, although *In a Green Pasture* had been translated to Hebrew. She'd also brought out a book of poems called *Flotsam*. The title seemed bleak, with its image of floating wreckage. I never read it. I leafed through it once, when it lay on Ruth's bedside table, but the poems seemed too religious for me, and made me uncomfortable. It won some kind of prize in Israel, though, and I heard that Essie now worked full-time as a writer, having long left the news agency.

As I said, 1982 was a lousy year. Essie was in my thoughts again because Israel's entry into Lebanon in June had released a barrage of anti-Israel media coverage, and a lot of it passed through my hands. Reuters reporting wasn't any more antagonistic than anyone else's, but I wanted Israel to remain upstanding, and it didn't seem that way at the time.

However, something happened that made the IAF jets lashing Lebanon as rockets rained down on Galilee seem like Guy Fawkes night in comparison with what was taking place in my personal life.

Ruth and I had been drifting further apart, and

we both knew it was happening. One night I worked late and, on a sudden impulse, dropped into a quiet restaurant on my way home. It was one of those dimly lit places where there's just enough light to read the menu but not the prices. The maitre d' seated me in a quiet corner since I was alone. Suddenly I looked across the room and there, unmistakably, was Ruth with a man I'd never seen before, their heads bent toward each other as they sipped their wine. There was no question in my mind that they were lovers.

I felt violently ill. For whatever reason, I had never been unfaithful in the twenty-four years of our marriage, and it had never occurred to me that Ruth might be playing around. We still shared a bedroom, and she was the one who always claimed she loved me more than I loved her. The guy wasn't even particularly attractive, a big florid man wearing a tweed suit and a loud tie. I wanted to knock his teeth in. Instead, I got up and walked out. But she'd seen me. Out of the corner of my eye I saw her startled gesture and her hand flying to her mouth to stifle the gasp of surprise.

I don't know how I drove myself home. I don't remember anything of the journey. The house was empty; Tiffany must have been at a friend's. All I remember was reeling into the study and taking a stiff drink, waiting for Ruth to come home. I could feel myself shaking as though I'd developed a fever.

I didn't have long to wait, maybe thirty minutes. She saw the light in the study and came straight in.

"I was going to tell you, Max. I was waiting for the right time."

"When is the right time to tell a man his whole life is a lie?" I asked bitterly. "Who the hell is he?"

"Wait, Max. Please, listen. When we first started going out, I told you I was getting over a relationship with someone." She didn't wait for my answer. "Well, I met him again recently."

"How recently?"

"Four months ago."

"You bitch!" I had to grip my hands, so strong was my impulse to hit her. "For four months you've been sleeping with this guy and putting on an act of a concerned, caring wife for me."

"No, Max. It didn't happen like that. It's only happened a few times."

"Is that supposed to make me feel better?" I said, pacing and dragging my fingers through my hair— I felt like pulling all of it out.

"Max, who are you kidding? You haven't cared for me in that way for years."

"Who says?"

"I say. Sure, we've gone through the motions. But I lost you a long time ago, if I ever had you." She fell into a chair, her head down. I couldn't tell if she was crying.

"What's that supposed to mean?"

She looked up at me, her eyes filled with tears. "We both know I was only second-best, right from the beginning."

"No, Ruth. It's not true. For twenty-four years you've been everything to me. I never looked at anyone else."

"Except Essie."

"You've got an obsession with Essie," I said halfheartedly.

"No, Max, you have the obsession. Do you think there wasn't one minute I didn't know you were still in love with her? That you were comparing me with her? That you would have gone to her in a minute, if she'd only raised her finger?" Again, she looked away.

Suddenly I felt the anger drain away and an immense weariness take its place.

"Ruth, what about the children?"

"They don't have to know. Nothing need change." She paused, then added, "He's married, too."

"Lovely!" This time I shouted. "Just lovely. What's his name?"

"What difference does it make?"

"I want to know his name."

"Raymond Gill."

I knew the name, of course. He was an art critic who believed that he was paid to criticize, and that only press agents said nice things.

"What are you trying to do, ensure a good review for your next show?" I said cruelly.

"That's unworthy of you, Max. Raymond and I lived together for a short time twenty-five years ago. We were going to be married, but he met someone else. I was terribly hurt, but I met you again soon afterward and was able to forget him. We met again by accident. I suppose I was feeling neglected, and he was very flattering, not just about my work, but about me. Women . . . I . . . need approval and affection, and God knows you weren't giving me any."

"Not to mention sex."

"It wasn't for the sex, Max, and you know it. I had moved to the periphery of your life. You simply weren't interested in me anymore. Raymond was."

"Interested enough to marry you? Are you going to ask me for a divorce?"

She reddened. "No, Max, that's not what this is about—stop!"

"Does his wife know?"

"No."

"I see. Just a dirty little affair, a bit of fun on the side."

I thought she was going to strike me, and I would have welcomed it—physical pain would have been so much more bearable than what was happening inside me. I knew I was a hypocrite; if Essie had agreed, I would have done exactly what Ruth had done. And my own self-serving logic would have allowed me to forgive myself on the basis that Essie was the great love of my life. I couldn't be so charitable about Raymond Gill.

"Do you want a divorce?" Ruth asked after a long silence.

"I don't know. It depends . . ."

"On what?"

"Are you going to go on seeing him?"

"No, I guess not," she said slowly. "I just did it on impulse, out of desperation."

"When and if you've cut all ties with him, ask me again. At the moment I need some distance from all of this."

"Are you going to tell the children?" she asked diffidently.

"Of course not. Why should they suffer? We'll go on with the charade you've been acting out so successfully for four months. But for the moment I'll be sleeping in the study; just say I'm not sleeping well. If it wasn't true before, it sure as hell will be now."

She made a tentative move toward me, and then thought better of it. She left the study, closing the door behind her.

*I*f life had been going sour before I discovered Ruth's infidelity, it was now close to unbearable. I seemed to have no reason to get up in the morning. Weekends were the worst, particularly when it was family time and we would keep up the pretense that everything in the garden was lovely, as the saying goes. Mealtimes were an endurance test, but I found that if I just asked the kids questions about their studies and social life, there'd be enough exchanges to mask the fact that Ruth and I didn't directly talk to each other.

During the week I'd leave for work while Ruth was still sleeping, and usually found an excuse to stay at the office late so we didn't have to have dinner together. She continued to go out in the evenings, but I didn't suspect her of continuing the affair. If she had told me she would end it, I believed her. In any case, affairs don't have to be conducted at night, and she really had no reason to stay at home—certainly not for my charming company.

Ruth may have been my consolation prize in the marital stakes, but I had truly loved her, and I felt betrayed. Even if it wasn't a great love affair, I had thought that we'd always be there for each other. Even if Essie had responded to my overtures, I don't believe I could ever have left Ruth for her; it would have been like an amputation. You live so long with someone and think you know them intimately, only to discover you don't know them at all.

I badly needed to be on my own for a while, but I was not in the mood for a holiday. An opportunity came up unexpectedly when a colleague came into my office one day and told me he was taking a break from an overseas assignment. Bob worked for Reuters and had just finished a stint as a member of the Commodore Battalion, the name given to the foreign reporters who frequented the bar at Beirut's Commodore Hotel, in the Lebanese capital.

Bob started telling me his view of what was happening there. When Israeli forces struck across the northern border on June 6, 1982, it was supposed to be a limited action against the PLO terrorists who had menaced the Galilee for a decade; in fact they called it "Peace for Galilee." It was now three months later and the operation was not only the focus of bitter criticism abroad, even the Israeli public were split in support of it. The media had written millions of words and shown thousands of feet of television footage, and most of it was devastatingly bad press for Israel.

After a month in Beirut, Bob was burnt out and needed a different assignment. It was then that the idea hit me that I could be his replacement. I had to get away, I needed a challenge, and I couldn't care less about the danger in my present state of mind. There was something else. The rise in sympathy for the Palestinians and the declining popularity of Israel, partly aided by its own conduct and appalling lack of public relations, was beginning to hurt me. There's a limit to how objective a journalist can be. I was Jewish, even if only minimally by Essie's standards, and I surprised myself by caring about Israel. It was rather like a family drawing together and closing ranks in times of crisis. You may think your brother is insane, but you'd knock the block off any stranger who would suggest it.

I'd been getting increasingly uncomfortable with the stories Bob was filing, and although they seemed

to be supported by all the other foreign correspondents, I couldn't believe that there wasn't another side
to it. Israel had already made one fatal error. They
had banned the press from the battlefield during the
first few days of fighting, resulting in grossly exaggerated accounts of Israeli destruction of the coastal
cities of Tyre and Sidon. Afterward, corrected and
much more accurate figures were issued, but the damage had been done. No one ever reads retractions
anyway. The truth was that Israel had made a great
effort not to hit untargeted buildings. Some reporters
had even written about the destruction of the town of
Damur, which had been caused by the PLO light-years
before, and when I checked our archives, I realized
how much sloppy reporting was going on.

I made my decision to do a stint in Lebanon
before discussing it with Ruth. I thought my going
away for a few weeks or even months would be very
welcome as far as she was concerned, but I must
have been a rotten judge of character, because, just
as I always misjudged Essie's reactions, so I misjudged Ruth's. We were alone after dinner, and perhaps my delivery may not have been polished or
suave, but she burst into tears. All I had said was:
"I'm going to be away for a while, Ruth. I'm replacing Bob Jarvis in Lebanon."

I waited for the tears to subside, more bewildered than anything else. "For God's sake, what's all that about?"

"This is to punish me, isn't it?" she said accusingly.

"Of course not. Don't be ridiculous."

"Yes it is. You'll be killed, and I'll be left to feel guilty for the rest of my life."

"I have no intention of getting killed, I can assure you, but if I do, I absolve you of any guilt. I'll put it in writing if you like."

"You're making fun of me!"

I was getting exasperated. "Ruth, you're being ridiculous. I am going to Lebanon as a correspondent for Reuters. I am not enlisting in the Israeli army, they have enough problems without me. I will be one of dozens of foreign correspondents there reporting the war. I'll stay at a hotel in Beirut, because that's where the PLO has shifted its base of operations. The only danger I'll be in is of becoming an alcoholic because foreign correspondents always drink too much. Otherwise, I'll be fine and perfectly safe."

The sobs had stopped, but she was still mopping her eyes. "You're not telling the truth," she insisted. "I know that newsmen have been intimidated, held hostage, even murdered there. Either that, or they've had to befriend Syria and the PLO, and write favorable stories if they value their lives."

I was amazed by her perspicacity and grasp of the facts. She was a highly intelligent woman, and I was always undervaluing her knowledge. I hedged. "Yes, that may be true. But I'm not going out on a limb. There are respected correspondents there from *Time* and *Newsweek;* Richard Cohen is there from the *Washington Post,* Nick Thimnisch, the columnist, even Tim Llewelyn from the BBC. They'd be pulled out by their bosses if they were in real danger; they're too good to risk."

"Just tell me something. If I hadn't had an affair, would you have taken this assignment, or would you have sent someone else?"

"It has nothing to do with that. Please believe me. I've more or less gotten over it," I lied. "No, if this is about anything, it's about being fifty-six. I have maybe nine years left before I'll probably retire—or be asked to. I suppose I want one last bit of excitement. I feel stale and old, and I need to do something a bit different before I'm put out to pasture."

"When will you go?"

"After the weekend. Now that Bob is back, we have no one there and that's where it's all happening right now. I should have sent someone to relieve him before he left, but all my best men are tied up, and anyway, it's somewhere I've always wanted to go— maybe not under these conditions—but Lebanon has an exotic sound to it, doesn't it? You know, 'the cedars of Lebanon.'" I was trying to make normalcy out of an insane situation. When she didn't answer, I babbled on. "Once they used to call it 'the Switzerland of the Middle East.' It's supposed to be beautiful."

"That isn't what they're calling it these days. There's so much slaughter, it's a wonder there's any population left."

In a way I was touched. Her hysterical outburst at least had assured me that my death would not have been a relief to her, that she did in fact want me to remain in her life despite her romantic episode. I felt myself soften toward her. "Ruth, I really will be okay," I assured her gently. "If you like, we can go away for the weekend—just the two of us—to that inn you like so much near Stratford." She looked to see if the invitation meant what it implied. I nod-ded, and she reached for my hand. It was a start of the healing process, at least. I hoped that being on my own for a while in the midst of a war might com-plete the peace process in my own marriage.

25

I went to Lebanon via Israel, but for once Essie was not on my mind, and not for one moment did I think of contacting her. All my thoughts were on the forthcoming assignment, and I felt an eagerness and excitement that I remembered from my days as a cub reporter.

Before we actually went into Lebanon, all the media people spent the night at an Israeli kibbutz on the border, called Gesher Haziv. A press center had been set up, and journalists, camera crews and broadcasters were milling around eating and drinking, joking, and making interminable phone calls. There were a lot of Israeli soldiers, too, and I was told these would be assigned to us as IDF liaison officers, and we would not be permitted to enter Lebanon without one of these "chaperones." I was given some

PR material marked "Strictly Confidential," and when I looked around, I saw that all the other journalists were holding the same press release. For some reason, I was vastly amused, and as I laughed with some guys I know from the *Jerusalem Post,* I felt all my years and cares starting to slip away. I felt young again, as though I were on the brink of a great adventure, which of course I was. I found myself a chair and read the PR material. It was about the work of the support units operating in South Lebanon on casualties, medical aid, food and water supplies, and relations with UNRRA, the Red Cross, Catholic Relief Services, and so on. We'd also been given a comprehensive map of the area and quite a thick book of briefing on the background. Before retiring, we were all asked to sign a form which stated that whatever might happen to us in Lebanon was our own responsibility, and we entered at our own risk. The same applied to the car I'd rented—a blue Peugeot with distinctive yellow Israeli number plates. It was sobering to sign such a document, as though this was not going to be such a carefree jaunt after all.

Before I went to bed, I made contact with an Israeli photographer, Avi, who'd be traveling with me, and the liaison officer provided by the IDF. His name was Eliezar, he informed me; he was in the

army reserves and this was his thirty-day *miluim,*
reserve duty. We had a few beers together, and I liked
him enormously. He was only about thirty-two, but
he was already a veteran of this army, where Israeli
boys were eighteen and nineteen, kids with baby
faces doing jobs most men never encountered in
their lives. I thought rather guiltily of my own two
sons and their pampered and privileged lives back in
London. Young as he was, Eliezar had also fought in
the 1973 Yom Kippur War nine years earlier, and had
served at least a month every year since, wherever he
was needed. There was nothing jingoistic about his
feeling for Israel; it wasn't a question of "my country,
right or wrong." There was a job to be done, and
Israel needed him, it was as simple as that.

Before I retired, I read some of the briefing material that had been given to me by Eliezar. It clarified
something that had been worrying me and which
Bob Jarvis's reports had failed to convey. Although
international law abhors the use of violence to
settle a conflict, it is sanctioned when a nation
needs to defend itself and its citizens from attack.
There seemed little question that the PLO intended
if possible to destroy the Jewish state. For the past
decade it had demonstrated this goal by a series of
murderous attacks on Israel's northern cities and

settlements from the sanctuary it had created for
itself in Lebanon.

The Americans had organized a truce a year earlier, in July 1981, but even though this had tem-
porarily put a stop to violations across the border,
the PLO continued in its military buildup in southern Lebanon. This posed a grave danger to those
Israelis living in the north, and it made normal life
impossible for them because of the ever-present
threat of attack.

What I couldn't understand was the Lebanese
government. For ten years they had allowed their
territory to be used as a base for acts of aggression
against a neighboring state, which was a violation of
the most basic precept of international law. They
could have appealed to the United Nations to prevent the situation, which they seemed quite unable
to control, but they didn't, although several times
they applied to that body to restrict Israel from
retaliating after it had been attacked.

These were the questions that filled my mind
before I went to sleep. Although in a few hours I
would be in a war zone, I felt more peaceful than I
had for months. I had something tangible with
which to get to grips instead of that dismal feeling
of failure that had been dogging me for so long,

crystallized in the failure of my marriage. Instead of the dead weight of apathy, I felt light with the anticipation of challenge—a job to do, free of any emotional entanglements. "Only people make you cry," someone once told me.

I slept that night—for the first time in a very long time—completely free of dreams.

After a very early breakfast, we crossed into Lebanon at 7 A.M. The country had been at war for eight years before the "Peace for Galilee" operation, but terrorist organizations had, in fact, been in Lebanon for fouteen years. The communal balance and the economy had been completely destroyed, yet there was physically little to show of this interminable conflict although I was told that 98,000 citizens had been killed and 225,000 wounded by the eight-year battle up to 1980, two years before Israel's incursion.

Again Lebanon was at war with Israel, but this time on Israeli soil. I don't know what I'd expected to see, but the first town we came to across the border was a surprise. Naqoura looked like something out of an old cowboy movie, a western-style shanty town where UNIFIL had its headquarters. It had a Silver Coast restaurant, a few stores, and even a "coiffure des dames," for the pretty Swedish nurses at SWEDMEDCO.

We were held up for a while since there was a convoy before us of thirty vehicles carrying medical supplies and ice cream in a mobile blood bank. The first twenty vehicles were Israeli front-wheel drive Magen David Adom ambulances, and the rest of the cars were filled with doctors and paramedics. They had taken on the ice cream in Nahariya, where Israelis had sent it as a gift to Lebanese children.

I used the opportunity to chat with a guy from the Dutch battalion. His smart blue beret went well with his blond hair and blue eyes.

"What are you doing here?" I asked him.

"I'm just a doorkeeper." He laughed. "I let people in and I wave them good-bye."

"What people?"

"Everybody," he said magnanimously.

"Nothing else?"

He thought for a moment. "I wish them luck. You, too!" he added.

No sooner had we got started than our car was pushed into the dust of the coastal road by an enormous Israeli armor-carrier loaded with a vast tonnage of captured ammunition and Russian T-34 tanks that looked as if they were left over from World War II. It took about half an hour to drive the twenty kilometers to Tyre along deeply rutted roads. It was a romantic location on a small bay with a marina for shipping vessels. It had an exotic skyline of minarets, spires, and domes, and I thought wistfully of how Ruth would enjoy painting it. The only sign of bomb damage was in the city center, but not a great deal, and life seemed quite normal on this Sunday morning. The shopping center was swarming with Lebanese, soldiers and journalists.

We stopped for a coffee at Patisserie Arabe, and Mr. Ramlawi, the proprietor, was beaming at the brisk business he was doing. Outside, a young boy was serving drinks and ice cream. Inside, the coffeehouse was high-ceilinged and exotic. We were brought Turkish coffee in tiny china cups and a mouthwatering selection of elaborate confections in colored marzipan. A ten-tier wedding cake dominated the glass display case.

Mr. Ramlawi nodded genially to me and Avi, but spoke to Eliezar, our liaison officer who was wearing an IDF uniform. "You are welcome in this country," he informed him. "When the terrorists were here, they would come into the shop, ten at a time, taking whatever they wanted—food, money, cigarettes. It is good that you got them out."

As we left I noticed some Hebrew lettering on his door. Eliezar told us it simply said "Open," and underneath it, the words *Baruch Ha'ba,* meant "Welcome!" I told Avi to photograph it, with Mr. Ramlawi, but the proprietor quickly moved away. I understood that if Israel lost, he might need to change his loyalties even more swiftly.

After our coffee I went to the public square to get some facts and figures on the local situation from the IDF spokesman. A middle-aged woman in a smart blue dress wearing a gold crucifix around her neck was plucking at his sleeve. "Please give me a permit to go to Israel. I must see my son; he is in the hospital." He directed her to wait. There was already a crowd gathered, some wanting to go to Israel, others wanting to go to Beirut where the PLO had broken the cease-fire and battles were raging again.

Having seen me talking to the spokesman, she must have imagined that I also had some kind of authority for she broke away from the group and came over to me. "My name is Sharia. Can you get me a permit?" she asked anxiously.

Sharia, who would have been pretty except for the lines of worry deeply etched around her eyes and mouth, had lived with her son in Tyre until the PLO made life impossible. The whole city had been under siege and the PLO took whatever they wanted violently, if they were refused. Like thousands of others, she fled north to Beirut in 1978, but the PLO began entrenching themselves there, too. She now felt that with Israel's presence it was safe to return to Tyre, so she had returned south. Her son, however, had been caught in the crossfire in Beirut before she left, and a helicopter had flown him to Nahariya in Israel.

"I've had a message that he will recover," she assured me. "But I want to visit him. Please help me."

I explained that I was just a British journalist with no "proteczia," no special connections whatsoever, but I promised to try.

"God will help me," she said piously, fingering her gold cross, "and Israel," she added as an afterthought.

I got all the details and passed them on to Eliezar, who said he would see what could be done. Avi took a photo of the group she had rejoined in the public square. It shows Sharia talking animatedly with another woman already feeling that I was going to perform a miracle for her. I had never felt more impotent in my life.

Eliezar told us there was something he wanted to show us just outside Tyre—the famous ruins of a Roman hippodrome and amphitheater from 13 B.C.E. which was used for chariot races and gladiatorial combat. The third largest of such structures in the world, it was magnificently well preserved. Behind the rows of ancient seats were cleverly concealed rooms built by the PLO terrorists. It was from this site that they had launched the rockets that had fallen on Nahariya. Israel knew this but had not bombed it in order to spare the ruins.

We went into some of the dark bunkers, filled with the ugly remnants of war: spent shells, tin helmets and PLO literature. There was a rancid stench of decay.

I felt claustrophobic, so while Eliezar accompanied

Avi to take photos, I went out into the sunshine. I was surprised to see an elderly man with a cane and a straw hat. His English was archaic, but he seemed anxious to show me around.

"Are you a guide?" I asked him.

"My name is Zyklowi. Follow me." He was neither friendly nor hostile, but he kept up a brisk monologue about the ruins and I almost had to trot to keep up with him. He ignored most of my questions. "See these flat stones? They were altars. Human sacrifice." I nodded, trying to insert questions about the present, not the past.

"Here you have three layers of civilization. Under this Roman road you can see the Greek, and this is Byzantine."

"I just wanted to ask you—"

"Here is aqueduct," he interrupted. "It carried water out five miles."

"The bunkers, Mr. Zyklowi, did you know about the bunkers?"

"I am guide," he said after a pause. "I work here." He would say nothing more, but waited expectantly. I fished around in my pocket and gave him a tip.

I looked at the beautiful arches silhouetted against a cloudless blue sky. From beneath them, rockets had spewed destruction on Israel's northern cities. I went to rejoin Eliezar and Avi. Mr. Zyklowi in his smart straw hat was still trotting around the arena, hoping for more visitors to whom he could explain the glory that was Rome.

We drove on to Sidon across the Litani River. The scene of other battles a few years earlier, the Litani area was new, looking strangely like a holiday resort. The banana plantations were splendid in the hot sun and soldiers of various allegiances wore bathing suits, with towels and underwear strung up to dry. Every building we passed seemed to be flying a flag. Over some it was Lebanese, the red and white stripes bordering the cedar tree reminding me of blood on a white handkerchief. A few houses displayed the Phalange flag, but many flew a white flag of surrender, too. However, Eliezar told me that the white flag merely signified that there was a virginal daughter of marriageable age whom her parents wished to marry off. It sounded a bit far-fetched to me, and I never did find out if it were true.

The road to Sidon followed the coastline, which was beautiful. The sea was shimmering, striped in bands of light aqua to deep indigo. I thought Sidon was rather like the Israeli port of Haifa. Sidon showed some war damage, with ugly bulks of unfinished buildings. What had once been an elegant villa was now nearly collapsed. The roof sat at a crazy, drunken angle, ludicrous atop the white facade and fluted columns. Through the open door I glimpsed high ceilings, crystal chandeliers, velvet drapes and a parquet floor.

A young man came out, but refused Avi permission to go upstairs to take pictures of Sidon. I asked him if he were glad that Israel had launched this operation. He shrugged. "War is not good, everyone suffers. True, we suffered more when the PLO were here. We turned ninety of them in last week who were hiding here, some to our Bishop, some to the Israelis. But when they finish the job, they, too, must go home," he stressed, pointedly looking at Eliezar's uniform.

"We'll be happy to," Eliezar answered.

The young man didn't smile. "Everyone must get out of Lebanon," he insisted. "PLO, Syrians, Israelis, UNIFIL, everyone!" I asked him if he were a Christian Phalange. He looked horrified. "I am a Shiite Moslem," he said coldly. Although I'd taken Avi along primarily as my photographer, he told me he'd been doing a lot of freelance work. "But the only shots I can sell to your British press," he said accusingly, "are those that seem to be anti-Israel. I've sold a few to the *Evening Standard,* but none to the other papers. They keep telling me, 'You're on their side,' which, of course, as an Israeli I am. But my camera doesn't lie. I've taken shots in Beirut, Damour, Tyre—this is my fourth trip to Lebanon. I had a magnificent picture that showed PLO head-quarters completely destroyed, yet so accurate was Israel's bombing capacity, that almost next door was a church left totally intact. Not one of the British papers would buy it."

He showed me some photos of the ruins in Damour with trees growing out of them, proof that they were bombed years ago and not during Israel's incursion. I took some of them, but I was not sure how successful I would be at getting them pub-lished. I was beginning to feel depressed at the double standard the world was showing toward this operation, and angry at the one-sided reports Bob Jarvis had been sending us.

Before we left Sidon we saw a strange sight. A young woman was directing a group of children sweeping the street in front of a building which had been hit by gunfire. She was blond and looked American, so I hopped out of the car to speak to her. I was wrong; she spoke only Arabic. Suddenly I was surrounded by children, all wanting Avi to take their photos with me. They laughed and chattered like happy children anywhere.

After the photos, a fat boy in a red T-shirt detached himself from the group and ran after me. He said his name was Honni and he was thirteen. He'd learned English at the National Evangelical School.

"Maybe you can help me find my uncle?" he pleaded. He told me the name. "Israeli soldiers took him away to Palestine a month ago. He do nothing. He own two shops in Sidon."

By this time Eliezar had joined me, and asked Honni if his uncle had just come from another country.

"He was a long time in Libya," the boy finally admitted. "But he not train to be a soldier. He work there for Italian company," he added with sudden inspiration. Eliezar jotted down all the details and promised to inquire. The children were still smiling and waving as we drove off, but I had a heavy heart. It would have been even heavier had I known what fate had in store for me before the day was through.

28

We were anxious to get to Beirut, but we'd been told that the fighting was heavy and we might not be allowed to enter. At any rate, we were starving, and we'd had one terrifying experience. We were almost caught in the crossfire of 155-mm cannons pounding over our head. A cow lay dead on the road in front of our car. With a shudder I realized that cow could have been us. Eliezar and Avi remained phlegmatic, but they were seasoned veterans of war. I suddenly realized that I wanted to get out of this assignment alive, and the odds were not so great that we would. It is easy to say you don't care about danger until you are faced with it. I was scared and was silently muttering a few prayers I'd managed to dredge up from my subconscious. I remembered an uncle who'd served in

World War I telling me the famous line of that war, that there were no atheists in the trenches. I could believe that.

Eliezar told us of a restaurant where we could get lunch on the beachfront. It bore the unlikely name of Sands Rock Beach. It was impossible to believe that war was so close. People sat on the terrace eating hummus and tahini or grilled chicken and chips, sipping cans of Coke and 7-Up. Pretty girls in bikinis flaunted their suntans, and the pool and beach below were crowded with Sunday pleasure seekers.

It was in the midst of lunch that I was almost paralyzed with shock. At a table behind us I heard someone questioning the waiter, who'd introduced himself to us as the proprietor's son, Pierre. He was wearing a ten-gallon hat like J. R. in *Dallas,* and was home on vacation from the University of Texas in San Antonio where he was studying hotel management.

I recognized the voice. "But what did you do when the terrorists beat you?" I spun around, and who should be there with these men but Essie, looking cool and beautiful. She was busily taking notes and didn't notice me. I couldn't believe it. What was the likelihood of my running into her here, on this day? It was as if some giant magnet in the universe was always pulling us together. How else could I explain all of our unlikely meetings?

I rose unsteadily and went to her table. She looked startled to see me in this wildly unlikely place, but then she smiled and motioned me to a chair next to her companions, as she carried on her interview.

"My father gave them a lot of money," Pierre answered her, "so they stopped. Another time they came to rob us, and I climbed out the window and hid until they were gone."

I introduced Eliezar and Avi, and Essie invited them to push our two tables together. She explained she was writing a series of cameos called "Voices of Lebanon" for the World Zionist Press Service and was traveling with her editor, a bearded man she introduced as Dan; her photographer, a tall auburn-haired guy named Douglas; and their assigned liaison officer, Shlomo. Eliezar and Shlomo recognized each other and were soon deep in conversation in Hebrew. The two photographers were comparing equipment and Dan decided to go for a swim.

Lebanon at that time was a mecca for journalists from all over the world, so it shouldn't have been such a shock to encounter Essie there—but it was, nevertheless. I knew she was a journalist as well as an author and poet from remarks Ruth had made when reading her letters. Every time I saw Essie, even now, at fifty-one, her desirability never ceased to draw me to her. Once again I noticed that she was wearing the pearl teardrop necklace. Following my gaze, she fingered it. Indeed, it made me feel like I, too, was always with her as she was with me; but maybe I was making too much of it. After all, I had given the necklace to her to wear.

"My good-luck charm," she said smiling, reinforcing my boyish hopes. "I always wear it on dangerous assignments."

"Do you have many?" I asked rather matter-of-factly.

"Living in the Middle East, most of them are dangerous." She laughed just the way Israelis do when speaking of the terrible danger they live with.

"But what are you doing here, Max? This is not your turf."

I mumbled something about replacing Bob Jarvis, but didn't elaborate.

"How is Ruth?"

I looked closely to see if her face betrayed any knowledge of what had happened between us, but I saw no indication that she knew.

"She's okay," I said uncomfortably.

"Isn't she frantic at your coming to a war zone? With the kids to consider?"

"Not such kids," I said ruefully. "Their lives are quite independent these days."

She had changed the subject and turned the intimate moment that had just passed between us—the gesture toward the necklace—into a polite series of questions. She was both present for me and utterly elusive, as always. Nevertheless, in my heart, I knew she was as thrilled to see me again as I her.

We could hear the sounds of battle coming from Beirut, and it seemed incredible that the Lebanese were swimming, eating and enjoying themselves, impervious to the war. We tried to analyze if they were people of a remarkably placid temperament or calloused, resigned, uncommitted, or merely fatalistic. The three million Lebanese comprised scores of different factions—Christians of seven sects, Sunni Moslems, Shiite Moslems, Mutawalis, Palestinians, and Druze—each spoke with a different voice and wanted different things.

Essie was also trying to get to Beirut, against the advice of her IDF officer, so we decided to travel in a convoy of two cars—she was in an army jeep—although what one could have done to protect the other, I have no idea. We went in front along some of the most abominable roads I've ever traveled on. For nearly a decade, an incessant stream of tanks and heavy armored vehicles had plowed up any semblance of road surfacing, and sometimes our wheels would roll into ruts two feet deep. Although the distance wasn't great, it was late afternoon when we reached Jazzine, to the east of Sidon. We were going on a roundabout route since at every checkpoint soldiers would turn us back from the road to Beirut.

We were high in the mountains. The road had climbed steeply past roadside madonnas of white plaster in blue gowns and gold haloes, past the university of St. Joseph. Below in the valley was a breathtaking view of silver-green olive trees, terraced grape vines, and the majestic biblical cedars of Lebanon.

Although the town had seen heavy fighting between the Syrians who set up ambushes and the Israelis, who sustained many losses, there was no sign of it this day. Life seemed so peaceful in this lovely village that wrongly appeared untouched by war. It was easy to understand now why Lebanon was called the Switzerland of the Middle East.

When we stepped out of our cars there was a Sunday afternoon promenade taking place near a small waterfall. Young girls in high-heeled sandals, lots of jewelery and makeup, were strolling in pairs, arms linked, past boys who eyed them appreciatively. One pretty girl was wearing a T-shirt that incongruously proclaimed in pink, blue and silver: "Sweet things remind me of you."

Essie was trying to talk to a little girl who was peeking at her between her fingers. She asked her name. When she made her understand, the child shook her black glossy curls and said, "Abir." She asked how old she was and she held up eight fingers, enjoying the game.

I tried to talk to a Lebanese policeman as handsome as a film star. He shook his head, only Arabic. After my greeting of *Marhaba,* and his reply of *Mar sala'am,* I'd exhausted my vocabulary. Nevertheless he agreed to pose for both Avi and Douglas near the waterfall.

Essie's editor said he wanted some coffee, so the seven of us filed into a coffeehouse. It was a mistake. Men were playing cards and backgammon and smoking *nargileh*—water pipes. By the sudden silence and cessation of activity, we knew we'd made some kind of faux pas. At first we thought it was due to the uniforms of Eliezar and Shlomo. Then we realized it was because of Essie. She was the only woman in the place, all the others were outside talking animatedly in the street.

Anyone but Essie would have left. The atmosphere

was not only uncomfortable, it was almost sinister. But she displayed her usual poise and sat down, so we all ordered coffee. The waiter served us with his face averted; the bill seemed unreasonably high.

Darkness began to fall just outside Beirut. The sun sat low in the sky, an orange disc with drifts of deep blue cloud floating across it. The light became a hazy blue and finally black. At every road junction someone yelled at us—Israeli, Phalange or UNIFIL forces—no one was happy to see us. They'd had their fill of journalists and I understood them. It was as if we were playing at war while they were risking their lives every minute.

We stopped when we got to Ba'abda, a once magical setting of splendid villas, where Israel's press center was located just a few kilometers from Beirut. Eliezar explained that they needed to take the pressure off a hard-pressed tank enclave close to the airport. Their guns were pointed at an apartment building where the PLO were entrenched. We were asked not to take any photographs, and Avi and Douglas both complied.

After being briefed, and with many warnings, we were allowed to continue to Beirut. My party went to the Commodore, and Essie's to the Alexandar, in the Achrafiah quarter. I had a sudden, terrible premonition that I'd never see her again—that one of us wouldn't make it. Before she climbed into the jeep, I drew her aside. "Essie, I love you," I said, brokenly. After our last meeting in London when she opened up a bit only to disappear, I now felt somehow freer to tell her how I felt. She squeezed my hand and her eyes filled with tears. Even though, "I know," was all she said in response, the unspoken reply I heard was, "And I love you."

The hotel was horrendous. The lift wasn't working, so I climbed up to the seventh floor and, when I reached my room, realized it wasn't worth the effort. I switched on the light and the shock from a loose wire shot me right across the room. It's a wonder I wasn't electrocuted. I decided to take a bath, but there wasn't a plug, so I settled for a shower. A thin trickle of tepid water left me even less refreshed than I was before.

It was strictly forbidden, but I decided to find a way to visit Essie on my own. I wasn't supposed to go anywhere without my liaison officer. I found Eliezar and Avi in the bar and told them I was turning in for the night. Then I snuck out a side door when their backs were turned.

I had a map, but no idea of distance, so I decided to walk. I was amazed at the shops; everything was

for sale at duty-free prices. I bought a kilo of cher-
ries and ate them as I walked. They were big, black,
and luscious, and their sweetness seemed to remove
some of the rancor that was choking me. Stores
were crammed with all kinds of electronic gadgets—
really cheap. There were also high-fashion clothes—
I thought guiltily of Ruth—and bottles of Johnny
Walker Red Label whiskey and Chanel No. 5 perfume at a fraction of the cost in London. Every
brand of American cigarette was available at give-
away prices.

Eventually I arrived at the Alexandar. It was much
farther than I'd anticipated and the ongoing sound
of gunfire was making me nervous. Essie's hotel was
even crummier than mine, and she wasn't in her
room. I found her with a crowd of press people up
on the roof. A German camera crew had their voice
camera rolling. The cease-fire was a joke.

I couldn't tell if she was pleased to see me or not.
I walked over to her and simply put my arm around
her waist; I was so happy to see her safe. She
accepted my gesture and together we looked down
from the roof on Beirut. Every now and again white
smoke billowed from the guns. Fire engines let their
sirens scream as they rushed off to put out yet
another blaze. The city was dying. I looked at Essie's

profile gazing down at Beirut and saw that two tears were sliding gently down her cheek.

"Can I stay with you tonight?" I asked her softly. I was surprised myself by my forwardness and the abruptness of the question, but I needed to be near her, if only now. She was a long time answering. I had the feeling that she wanted me as much as I wanted her. Finally, she whispered, "No, Max. We can't." I nodded silently; I wasn't surprised, just sad once again. We continued to stand there, close to each other. It was almost dawn when I left and took a taxi back to the Commodore.

I had many questions to grapple with in the days that followed. My path did not cross Essie's again. I sent back regular reports of a factual nature—that's what I was there for. I knew Essie's stories would be colored by her belief in Israel's right to be there, but I couldn't allow myself the luxury of expressing personal feelings.

The amount of PLO weaponry that had been found in southern Lebanon during the operation and already inventoried was staggering: 4,000 tons of ammunition; 144 vehicles; 12,506 small arms; 516 heavy arms such as rocket launchers; plus all kinds of communication and optical instruments. These were facts, and Eliezar explained to me that it would take eighty trucks working every day, a full month, to cart it all back to Israel.

I couldn't imagine what the Israelis would do with the five thousand terrorists they were holding in various military police installations. I was allowed to talk to some of them through interpreters—they were Jordanians, Egyptians, Algerians, Libyans and Syrians. I also discovered a few from Bangladesh, Pakistan, Sri Lanka, Somalia, Mali, Austria, Kuwait and Iran.

I also saw with my own eyes how all the weaponry had been smuggled into Lebanon by the PLO. A lot of it had come inside crates marked as agricultural spare parts (for tractors and bulldozers), medicines bearing the insignia of "Red Crescent," crates marked as canned tomatoes and matchboxes.

The crates marked spare tractor parts from North Korea contained 107-mm Katyusha shells. The IDF let Avi take photos, but I did not know how many would actually be published. The anti-Israel feeling was running high. Since June 6, when Israel had struck across the northern border in what they originally presented as a limited action against the PLO, the days had turned into weeks and then to months. The prolonged shelling of Beirut may have been a necessary tactic, but it turned world media against Israel even more. Prime Minister Menachem Begin remained mute throughout most of the campaign, and the cabinet ministers who did try to articulate Israel's case were woefully inadequate.

There were a lot of things bothering me. There were so many journalists there, but only a few of them were experts with any real knowledge of the conflict. Some of them were so raw and uninformed that they couldn't tell a Druze from a Druid, as the current joke went in Lebanon. But it was far from funny. Their misrepresentation was harmful. Someone would throw out a greatly exaggerated figure of casualties and others would echo it without question. Editors wanted sensational stories, and the media were only too happy to supply them, truthful or not.

The double standard that was showing up in reporting by even seasoned journalists worried me enormously, and I spoke of it to the correspondent from the *Washington Post*. Arab atrocities were being ignored while Israel's every action was harshly censured. "Israel asks to be measured by a higher moral standard," I was told.

I didn't think it was true. What was true was that it had higher standards of political morality, and it was engaged in a struggle for survival with enemies who didn't fight fair. I knew that was what Essie would say—and write. Her editor would publish it, but it would be read by Jews around the world. Mine would probably not.

I called Ruth one night and after a very long time managed to get through. She sounded anxious, but I reassured her everything was okay. She gave me news of the children. I didn't know whether to mention Essie or not. It was a Catch-22 situation. If I didn't tell her, and she found out later, she would think I'd gone to Lebanon for an assignation with Essie. As far-fetched as it sounded, Ruth could believe this. If I did tell her, the reaction might be worse. I decided, "Here goes nothing!"

"You'll be surprised when I tell you whom I met here." There was a crackling of static on the line.

"What did you say?"

"I said you'll be surprised—"

"I can't hear you."

"Never mind, it's not important."

"Take care of yourself!" she yelled.

"Sure," I answered. "You, too," I added before hanging up.

$\mathcal{T}$he hardest question I had to ask myself both personally and as a reporter was, what were Israel's real aims? First it was the forty kilometers business, then the entrapment and liquidation of the PLO. Eliezar said that Israel was keeping its army there to help Lebanon get back on its feet. But was that what Lebanon wanted? Everyone seemed to hate Israel by this point: the humiliated Moslems, the suspicious Druze, the hostile Christians. . . . I tried to get more facts for our readers, but always seemed to come up against a brick wall.

Lebanon itself continued to fascinate me. The contrasts were unbelievable. Life went on regardless of the fighting. It was still a beautiful and colorful country where rhododendrons, hydrangea, flame trees and canna lilies could be seen everywhere. We spent a day in Damour, south of Beirut on the coast. Here was the worst bomb damage I'd seen, even worse than Beirut, but most of it was from the civil war in 1976 when the PLO slaughtered one hundred Christians a day to make an example of them. It seemed strange to see Israeli Egged buses driving along the streets. Even stranger were the Ferris wheels—signs of a previous life when the air resounded with children's laughter. Today the wheels stood immobile—no more laughter, no more music.

I tried to call Essie at the Alexandar, only to be told she had gone back to Israel. I decided I'd had enough, too; I'd been there three weeks—the same time as Bob Jarvis—and I was burned out. But I felt satisfied with the stories I'd been filing—they were factual and as objective as I could make them—and I hadn't succumbed to the media sport of Israel-bashing in any of them.

I went down to the bar for a much needed nightcap and was surprised to run into Dan, Essie's editor. "Wouldn't have expected to see you here, Dan. I thought you were all packed up and gone." I was glad to see someone connected to Essie. Maybe she was still around.

"I have a few loose ends to tie up. You know how it is. Nothing is ever over."

"Is Essie with you by any chance?"

"Oh, no, she's back and busy."

"Right. Let me buy you a drink," I offered, a bit disappointed.

After we'd had a few, my lips were quite loosened and I found myself wanting to talk to Dan about Essie. I don't know what I was hoping for. "You're fortunate to be working with Essie, she's such a talented writer and journalist. I always knew she would be," I said, wandering off into my own thoughts.

"She is extraordinary, Max. Talented. Smart. Lots of integrity. She's the best there is. A fascinating woman. But, and I hope you don't mind my saying this, there's a loneliness to her, you know. I don't understand it. She's so lovely and all. But she's so private, so remote."

I started wondering if Dan himself had a crush on Essie, too. "Yes. She's very compelling. There's no question about that. Terribly compelling," I said, immediately ordering another round of drinks. Suddenly, I didn't feel like talking much.

"Max, are you okay?"

"Sure, no problem," was all I could say. I knew I'd fall apart if I spoke anymore. And with that I said good night and went up to my room.

"Listen, my friend," Dan said before I disappeared. "Some things, no matter how good they
seem to be in some respect, were not meant to be.
We have to accept that."

I smiled and nodded. Had he sensed correctly my
feelings about Essie? What did he know? Who had
taught him this lesson, I wondered.

I had mixed feelings about going home. I knew I
needed a bit more time, and I wanted to spend it in
Jerusalem. As we left, darkness began to fall. We
were on the road to Nabatiye—a terrible road fit
only for donkeys. Soon it was completely dark, and
we were not allowed to drive after the curfew. We
were speeding, trying to reach the Israeli border in
time, but we didn't make it. We were stopped and
shouted at by soldiers at every checkpoint.

Eventually we crossed the border and began the
long drive back to Jerusalem. Avi was driving,
Eliezar was asleep. The night was silent and filled
with stars. It was hard to believe I was in a country at
war—a strange experience—and I tried to sort out
my impressions. The only sounds I heard were the
voices from Lebanon repeating the same words like
a rerun of an old movie.

It was already the middle of the night when we

reached Jerusalem—a sultry midsummer night in
August. I wanted very much to talk to Essie because
I knew I wouldn't sleep. I seemed to have lived a lifetime in the past few weeks, and because she had
been through similar experiences, I felt a compul-
sion to discuss it with her. There was nothing
romantic in it, but if I'd called her at 3 A.M. she
probably would wisely figure out there was. She was
living in Yemin Moshe. I decided to splurge and
booked myself into the nearby King David Hotel,
the most expensive, and certainly the most elegant,
hotel in Jerusalem.

The contrast with the crummy accommodation
I'd had in Beirut couldn't have been more marked.
I luxuriated in a hot bath and used all the toiletries
the hotel had provided—even the bubble bath.
Afterward, I thought I smelled like a pansy so I had
a shower and scrubbed away as much of the fragrance as I could manage. I tried to sleep until they
began serving breakfast at seven, but it was a fitful
sleep and not at all restful. I kept wanting to phone
Essie, but resisted the temptation until a reasonable
hour.

I was the first in the dining room and felt very conspicuous and greedy. It was a smorgasbord, and although I'd heard a lot about Israeli hotel breakfasts,

this one had to be seen to be believed. At home, often as not breakfast would consist of a cup of coffee and a cigarette. I circled the table, gazing in sheer awe at the display. There was a choice of several breakfast cereals, to be taken with milk, prunes or fruit compote. There were at least eight kinds of cheese and ten kinds of salad. There was pickled herring and matjes herring fillets, plump, pink and inviting. There were boiled eggs and fried eggs and scrambled eggs. There was toast, white bread, brown bread, bagels and croissants. There was yogurt and dairy products in all colors and flavors.

I heaped a plate with as much as I could fit. When I was halfway through eating it suddenly occurred to me that the sensible thing to have done would have been to invite Essie to join me for breakfast; it probably would have been a treat for her to eat at the King David and certainly would have doubled my enjoyment. "Too little too late," seemed to characterize all my actions where Essie was concerned.

I was more than replete, but I went back to refill my plate with some of the delicacies that hadn't fit the first time around. A few other guests were drifting in by this time, and I didn't feel so conspicuous or conscious of the waiter's scrutiny. I was glad to see that I wasn't the only greedy one; everyone was tackling heaped plates and looking regretful that they couldn't manage more.

I had decided not to call Essie until 8:30; it was a kind of self-discipline I'd imposed on myself. I got hold of a copy of the *Jerusalem Post* and settled in one of the leather armchairs in the lounge, feeling like a millionaire. It was August 21, and the headlines reported that the PLO had begun to withdraw from Beirut. I had left just hours ago, yet it seemed another world.

Back in my room I dialed Essie's number. She answered on the third ring.

"It's me," I said idiotically—always the brilliant conversationalist where Essie was concerned.

"Max?"

"I got back last night."

"Where are you?"

"In Jerusalem. At the King David Hotel. Are you free?"

"Not really," she said regretfully. "I'm just going out to do an assignment."

I'd forgotten that Israelis started work when normal people were still in bed. Everyone was in their offices by eight, and some of the food shops were open at six. I could easily have called hours earlier.

"When will you be free?"

"Not till about six. How long are you staying?"

I wanted to say it depended on her, but knew she would feel pressured. "I have some things to do, a few days maybe."

"I'd like to see you, Max." But she switched gears as if afraid of what was being unleashed between us. "Ruth must be so relieved to know you're safe."

I was appalled at myself. I hadn't even thought of contacting my wife since arriving in Jerusalem.

"Yes, she is," I lied. "Will you have dinner with me?"

"Yes," she answered softly. "Where will I meet you?"

"I'll pick you up," I said, hanging up quickly before she could change her mind.

I felt guilty about Ruth after the conversation, and sat in my room wondering what to do. If I called to say I was out of Lebanon, she'd expect me to come straight home. If I said I needed a few days holiday somewhere, she'd want to join me. If she knew I was in Jerusalem, she would know it was because of Essie.

I hadn't thought about Ruth at all during the weeks in Lebanon. Maybe I was still angry about her affair and this was how my subconscious was handling it. Maybe it was because of the proximity of Essie. I had no way to justify my behavior. I knew I was behaving badly; I couldn't stop myself—wouldn't—but I decided that discretion was the better part of valor, and I would wait a few days to contact Ruth and tell her that I was safely out of Lebanon. From her point of view, Jerusalem was, no doubt, a lot more dangerous.

I had about ten hours to fill before picking up Essie and no clear idea of what to do. I decided to go to Beit Agron—Journalists' House—a center for foreign correspondents with facilities, including translations of all the editorials from the Hebrew press and post office boxes to leave messages. Although I saw the names of a few colleagues I recognized from London, I still felt restless; there was no one I really wanted to contact.

I wandered aimlessly around the buildings and found myself in the area of the Military Censor's room. There were quite a few reporters having their copy screened by soldiers. One attractive young woman in uniform was refusing to put the official stamp of approval on some Scandinavian's copy and he was red with anger. But she was adamant, insisting that certain lines had to be taken out.

Back in the corridor, I heard more journalists with American and Irish accents phoning in copy to their editors. One guy was speaking with unbelievable rapidity in French. I went to have a coffee and heard two journalists laughing uproariously.

"So Nicaragua says they are cutting ties with Israel over its siege of West Beirut. What ties?" said one laughing.

"Must be three years since the Managua government had any contact with Israel," his companion replied.

"They don't have a diplomatic mission there and for sure Nicaragua doesn't have one here."

I wanted to join them to say that while I was in Beirut I'd learned that the PLO was training two hundred Sandinista guerrillas and Nicaraguan pilots, but they seemed to be enjoying each other's company so much I felt it would be an intrusion. When a young woman joined them, they switched to Hebrew so I left.

It was brilliant sunshine outside, and I decided to walk in the Old City and maybe buy a present for Essie. On second thought I realized she probably wouldn't be interested in objects from the Arab market and decided on some gifts for my family instead; buying for them made me feel a little less guilty about what I was doing in Jerusalem.

I went through the Jaffa Gate, captivated by the exotic atmosphere. There seemed to be quite a few tourists, mostly in groups being led by tour guides.

I tried to look as inconspicuous as possible, but an obese Arab, his hair plastered with brilliantine, spotted me immediately. "You have dollars to exchange?" he asked politely.

"No, I'm not an American."

"Sterling perhaps? I give you a good price."

I decided I might need more Israeli currency if I was going to buy gifts, so I followed him into a little shop at the top of David Street, which had "Official Money-Changer" lettered in gold on the window which also contained a variety of curios—olive wood crucifixes and painted icons for the Christians, embroidered yarmulkes and brass menorahs for the Jews. Business is business, I thought to myself.

We made the transaction. I was quite satisfied, as I'd seen what the banks were giving in the morning paper and I'd done better than that, and also better than the rate posted at my hotel. The proprietor even offered me a cup of Turkish coffee, which I declined as graciously as I could.

The souk was a feast for the senses as I made my

way down the steep winding streets, moving to one side every now and again to allow a laden donkey to pass me. Hawkers were offering mint tea on little brass trays, freshly baked bagels topped with sesame seed, and boxes of Turkish delight, highly perfumed and colored mauve. I paused at one of the stores to look at sets of carved camels, when a young boy, no more than fourteen, grabbed my sleeve.

"You would like to meet my sister, she is very pretty?" he whispered.

I shook him off. "No," I said gruffly.

He narrowed his streetwise eyes, looking at me speculatively. "Maybe my brother?" he offered hopefully.

To get rid of him, I went into the store and started examining the jewelry. "I'd like something for my wife," I said loud enough for him to hear. I let myself be talked into some rather garish Eilat-stone earrings, which I thought Tiffany might find fun, and a silver filigree hand on a thin chain that the storekeeper assured me would keep away the Evil Eye, for Ruth.

When I was sure the youth had given up on me, I continued my meandering, enjoying the sights and smells that assailed me. I stopped at another stall and bought a chess set of ivory and inlaid mother of pearl for Jeremy and a nargileh for Simon; I thought a water pipe would appeal to his offbeat sense of humor. I also bought a rather beautiful Persian rug after half an hour of haggling. I knew I had still overpaid but I could picture it on the floor in my study and I suddenly wanted it desperately.

By the time I'd reached the bottom of the street, I'd added two *djellabah* for Ruth and Tiffany—long loose gowns in fine linen—Ruth's was white, embroidered in silver, and Tiffany's was turquoise. I was overburdened by then with all my parcels, but I suddenly saw the perfect gift for Essie and I knew I had to have that, too. It was a fruit bowl of hand-painted Armenian pottery, beautifully shaped, with deep carnelian blue flowers and lacy green leaves scattered over the white background.

I then had to reclimb the steps, and I was out of breath when I got back to the Jaffa Gate. I took a taxi to my hotel even though the distance was short. I had a sudden premonition that there would be a message at the desk from Essie saying that she couldn't meet me after all, but the clerk just handed me my keys with a smile.

I still had several hours to fill, so I lay down on my bed meaning to close my eyes for just fifteen minutes, but the morning's activities must have

exhausted me because I fell into a deep sleep. I
dreamed I was making love to Essie, and it was
unbearably sweet, but all of a sudden I looked at her
face and it was Ruth. I woke up with a start, confused, and a feeling of grief seemed to wash over
me. More than an hour had passed since lying
down. I took another shower to wash off any linger-
ing fragrance from the morning's bubble bath, all
the while trying to analyze my dream. Ruth often
interpreted her dreams for me, but I naively
assumed interpreting dreams was something only
women did. I never dreamed or, if I did, I didn't
remember them. However this dream was so vivid
and so disturbing, I couldn't put it out of my mind.
In the end I attributed it to guilt at being in
Jerusalem without Ruth knowing.

My plans for the evening were vague. I could not
expect the moment of great intimacy with Essie I
had so hoped and longed for. I knew it was wrong.
I also knew it might endanger everything that was
important in my life. Nevertheless, it happened
every time I was near her. I simply couldn't avoid it.
All I was sure of was that I wanted to be near Essie,
just to look at her and to share our experiences in
Lebanon. I also wanted to know something of her
life. I had managed quite successfully to put her

out of my mind while she was married; perhaps I could forget her because she was connected to someone else.

I knew it was stupid, but suddenly I felt protective of her again. After all, she lived alone and had no children and, although it hurt me to admit it even to myself, she was middle-aged. I remembered what Dan had said about her loneliness back at the bar in Lebanon. As far as I knew, there were no significant men in her life and, although she was a successful writer, that didn't always mean that one accumulated enough money to guarantee security. As a kibbutznik, I assumed Adi had not been able to give her either a settlement or alimony when they divorced. I'd accumulated quite a lot of money over the years, more through good luck than good management, and I couldn't bear to think that she might be living a life of privation or penury.

When it was five o'clock, and I couldn't stretch out the time in the coffee lounge any longer, I decided to stroll to her home, having a look at Yemin Moshe on the way. The sun was still shining, but the heat had lifted and the sun felt like a blessing on my face and arms. "Jerusalem, the golden" may be a hackneyed phrase, but wherever the sun touched the mass of gray stone out of which

Jerusalem was fashioned, it did indeed soften the starkness to molten gold.

The entrance to Yemin Moshe was through a park, and there couldn't be a more delightful approach to the place where Essie lived. Scarlet geraniums and red roses contrasted with all the different shades of green in the trees and leaves and grass. There were winding lanes and cobblestone steps and whitewashed, shuttered homes that one associates with Mediterranean countries. I could understand why there were signs pointing to so many artists' studios; the area seemed charged with creative energy. I sat on the low wall near the windmill, which had once served as a flour mill. A fellow countryman, Sir Moses Montefiore, had built it to provide productive work for the residents of this first quarter outside the Old City walls. A plaque informed me that the long, low dwellings were built by Judah Touro of New Orleans. A few people were sitting on the veranda of Mishkenot Sha'ananim and I wondered if they were famous because I knew this was a kind of guest house where the mayor invited artists, writers and musicians to stay.

The shadows were beginning to lengthen when I found Essie's address, although it was still light and the air was caressingly warm. Like all the other houses, hers was charming. A clay pot on the fence was filled with ivy, which spilled down and softened the stone, its green tendrils wandering into every crevice.

Ridiculous as it sounds, it took courage for me to press the doorbell. Actually, I didn't find anything to press. Instead, a rope hung down, and when I pulled it, chimes reverberated from inside, musical and somehow fragile. Even though Essie would be expecting me, I still felt like a callow youth setting himself up for rejection.

But as the chimes died away, I heard the light click of her heels on the tiled floor hurrying to open the door, and her smile was warm and welcoming. She took both of my hands in hers and drew me inside. "I can't tell you how happy I am that you're here."

"Are you?"

I searched her face to see if she were just being polite, but found no evidence, just genuine pleasure. It was like I'd been holding my breath, and could suddenly let it go and relax. She led me into one of the most delightful rooms I'd ever seen. It was simply furnished, certainly nothing expensive, but the effect was stunning.

Like most Jerusalem homes I'd visited, the floors were tiled and uncarpeted, giving a cool, clean appearance. Her furniture was simple wicker, but with lots of cushions, upholstered in bright floral cotton. Plants in wrought-iron containers stood in the corners, and there were lots of paintings. On the low glass-and-wicker coffee table stood a black vase filled with a most unusual combination of flowers, roses in white, pale gold and pink teamed with purple bougainvillaea, flaunting itself like a scarlet woman. I would never have dreamed of putting such flowers together, but they looked wonderful. Essie had an unerring sense for such things. She was wearing a lilac dress that contrasted beautifully with her silver hair, and just looking at her in that setting was a feast for all my senses. She was also wearing the teardrop pearl.

"Am I glad to see you? Why should you doubt it?" she finally asked. I wanted to tell her exactly what I had been thinking about, why I doubted her, but it seemed as though it would come out all wrong.

"I'm afraid to say things to you, Essie. I always feel like we're speaking different languages. You've confused me so much over the years."

"I know. . . . I know," she whispered, bending her head down, as if in shame or regret, I didn't know which. "Max, I feel so much for you. I always have. I don't know what to say."

With this she took my hand. She felt so close. I wanted to take her in my arms, to kiss her lips, to tell her how I loved her, that there was hardly a moment in my life when I hadn't thought of her. Yet I knew she could read the longing in my eyes.

"Max, I've missed you so much. I remember, as if it were yesterday, the way we were together in London. I can't forget. Never. But, much as I want to, we could never be lovers. We couldn't do this to Ruth. Besides, it would change our lives completely. I don't know if either you or I could live with that."

For the first time Essie looked as desperate as I felt. She was completely open, finally. Did she live as I had, thinking of me, wanting me, wondering if her life could have been different, better?

I thought for a moment, and decided to share my other grief with her. "Ruth has been having an affair."

She was shocked. She looked at me intently, and I watched as she nearly dropped her teacup. "Max, I'm so sorry. I don't know what to say. I can't believe it. Ruth worships you."

"Once, maybe, not anymore." I didn't mean to sound pathetic, but somehow it came out that way. I shrugged. It was a gesture I'd only recently developed. It seemed more expressive than words, especially when you weren't sure how much pain your voice would reveal. I cleared my throat. "I probably deserved it."

"I doubt if she did it to punish you," she said softly.

"I don't know why she did it. Maybe for a bit of excitement, maybe to fight against growing old—who knows?"

"I think I know."

"Perhaps I don't want to hear it."

"It's up to you."

She picked up her teaspoon, and rotated it slowly in her cup, avoiding looking at me.

"Max, you were never fair to Ruth."

"Rubbish," I said angrily. "I gave her everything, a wonderful home, a comfortable life. She was free to come and go. I never questioned her. I provided a housekeeper, so she could paint, and a nanny when the kids were small."

"That's not what I'm talking about. Ruth always knew how you felt about me. How do you think she felt? She obviously wanted you to love her and her only. Knowing your husband loved someone else would be devastating for any wife."

"It wasn't like that. Once you were married, I tried never to think about you, and most of the time I succeeded. Even if I wasn't 'in love' with Ruth, I did genuinely love her. My life on a day-to-day basis revolved around her and the kids. I wouldn't have dreamed of doing anything to hurt her."

"What about the day I visited you at Reuters, last time I was in London? You wanted to make love to me then."

"Yes, I did, and I always have. How can I deny that? I wanted to be close to you. But I never made Ruth feel unloved or uncared for. It's just, well, what can I say, Essie? I can't stop loving you. Maybe we could have found some way to be together without Ruth knowing."

"Max, you know that would never work. She'd know. And that wouldn't have been enough for us."

"Then how come I didn't know about her?"

"You should have, if you cared enough."

I let it pass. "You only mentioned two of us."

"I would be hurt the most of all."

I waited, hoping for, yet dreading, what might come next.

"You see, Max," she continued, looking straight into my eyes, "I have always loved you, too. But once I came to Israel I couldn't leave. When I left Adi, I thought of nothing but you. I kept trying to imagine us together. Where would we live? How could I keep what had become so important to me, my religion and my city, Jerusalem, and have you, too? I knew I couldn't, no matter how much you said you would change for me. I know that doesn't work. There would be resentment and . . . I don't know . . . so much. How do you choose between the man you love and how you want to live? Why do we have to make such horrible decisions, Max?"

And with that she wept. I could say nothing. The pain for both of us ran so deep.

"Has it made you happy? Or are you lonely?"

"Yes to both," she admitted, tears streaming down her cheeks now. "But it was my destiny, it was meant to be. I'm not happy; I doubt if I ever have been. But I think I've achieved something—fulfillment."

We were quiet after that. There didn't seem much to say. I was filled with a bittersweet sadness, brought about by her confession of love. I wasn't ready to talk about going out for dinner, it seemed too prosaic, although that was ostensibly the reason I was there. I tried one more time.

"Essie, if we just spent these few days together, making love . . ."

She shook her head. "And when they were over? Then what? What will we do with still more beautiful memories? As long as I've never known what it is like to sleep in your arms, I can live without it. I don't think I could let you go after having you so close to me."

I wanted to say: "I'll leave Ruth. I'll ask for a divorce. I'll live in Jerusalem." I had enough money for my family to continue a comfortable life and for me to retire. But the words stuck in my throat. After all these years, I was the one who wasn't ready. She squeezed my hand and looked at me. "Max, don't. You don't mean it, and it's not what's meant to be." She took a deep breath and, in typical Essie fashion, pulled herself together and changed the subject. "Well, what about that dinner you promised me?"

Perhaps she'd read my mind. Somehow it seemed she always knew that no matter how much we loved each other, we weren't destined to be together.

We went to a restaurant that had been converted from an abandoned Arab stone house on the outskirts of Jerusalem. Essie had chosen it, and I loved it. Narrow paths with uneven steps meandered through gardens of grapevines and gnarled olive trees, with sudden splashes of color from geraniums or wild violets. We chose an outdoor table lit by candlelight and where we could glimpse the stars through an overhead tracery of leaves supported by a trellis. The terrace where we ate overlooked the valley and the road to Tel Aviv. The cars on the streets were tiny dots of light moving downhill on our left, and the perfume of lemon trees, left to grow wild, wafted up from the valley below, and the scent of orange blossoms felt close.

The conversation in Essie's lovely home seemed

to have exhausted us emotionally and, at first, we talked very little. But it was not an uncomfortable silence. Even if we had never become lovers, we were still very old friends and that alone lent an intimacy that was a kind of enchantment. Over a delicious meal of Eastern food and grilled, succulent meats and highly spiced piquant vegetables, we gradually resumed a conversation, beginning with our experiences in Lebanon. "The press is so biased, so anti-Israel," she complained.

She told me of an incident that had happened in Damour. "There was this German TV crew filming war damage from at least ten years before Israel's incursion. They were trying to pass it off as something that had happened in the last few days. Right next door, there was an Israeli soldier in a house that had been abandoned watering the garden so that the trees and flowers wouldn't die. I asked them to be honest, to turn the camera on that instead. They just laughed at me. 'Don't you know, lady, that good news is no news,' one of them laughed. He's probably right. I couldn't sell the story to general media either," she said bitterly.

"What are you going to do with your life now, Essie?"

She hesitated. "It may sound boastful, but I've

made a name for myself in Jerusalem. I'll continue to write for the WZPS—they syndicate my work in 120 Jewish newspapers. I suppose it's just preaching to the converted. But non-Jews read my books, and I'm writing one about Lebanon; my publishers are interested. And my poems are starting to appear all over the world. I've had an offer to be scholar-in-residence next year at an American college, but it would be hard for me to leave Jerusalem."

"Why, Essie? What holds you? You weren't born here."

"No, that's true, and I almost never go back to Australia—just to see family, once every five years or so. But every time I leave Jerusalem, it's almost an amputation. I have such a feeling of belonging, and such a deep abiding love. I can leave for a few weeks, but longer than that becomes a deprivation. My soul belongs here," she said simply, and from her it didn't sound like an affectation; it was a plain statement of fact, which I could accept at face value.

She didn't attempt to analyze or explain it. And though every time I read anti-Israel propaganda or thought about the Holocaust, I identified more with being Jewish, there was no way I could feel at home in Israel as Essie did. It was too ancient, too biblical. Although there were times London grated on me, I could not imagine being far from there too long. I always find myself swallowing an unaccustomed lump of sheer emotion upon hearing the national anthem. I am British, by birth and by conviction. Judaism is my religion, and I like some of the rituals, which are comfortable and warmed by childhood memories.

Essie had none of those memories; her childhood was almost devoid of rituals, and yet she had been able to take this religion and make it her whole life. It seemed more than a matter of faith. It was a kind of obsession. In a way, it was a magnificent obsession, for it compensated for lack of a husband, children, even lovers—at least as far as I knew.

It took enormous chutzpah, but I decided to ask her anyway. "Essie, since your divorce, have you had any relationships?"

She smiled. "Very delicately put. What you mean is, have I been sleeping with anyone?"

I instantly regretted the question, because if she had, I didn't want to know. "I almost did," she confessed. "I was very attracted to one man, purely in a physical way. Maybe it was because he reminded me of you."

The "almost" piqued my interest. "And?"

"And nothing. He was a poet—very bad poetry, by

the way. When I let my attraction to him become a bit obvious, he told me he was gay."

"And he looked like me?"

"Just the eyes." She laughed. "You have beautiful eyes." I wasn't sure if I believed that she hadn't had lovers. She was a beautiful, sensual, desirable woman, and a woman who had an appetite for life. If she was covering up, I was grateful to her for sparing my feelings. She was quite clever and I regretted even putting her in that position.

We decided to walk back to Yemin Moshe, although it would take us about an hour. We were mellowed by the food and the wine and the balmy evening, and neither of us wanted it to end.

We climbed the hill that took us back to the entrance to Jerusalem, still busy with cars leaving and returning to the capital. We walked back along Jaffa Road, an ugly yet endearing thoroughfare. Crowds were still pouring out of Egged, the central bus station, coming back from visits to other cities less weighted with history and sobriety than Jerusalem. Many of them were soldiers—girls and boys with rifles slung over their shoulders—some coming home on leave, lines of weariness etched onto their young faces. I pitied them and was proud of them, yet at the same time I was thankful my children would never be among their ranks. Then I felt guilty for the thought.

Some of the buildings we walked past were grimy and gray, their shutters badly in need of paint. Others were new, and their very newness seemed almost an insult to the antiquity of Jerusalem. We hardly spoke, unless Essie wanted to point out something to me. I felt very peaceful, as though all kinds of unresolved tensions had finally dissolved. I could enjoy Essie without possessing her; I could admire Jerusalem as a guest, with no obligation toward her. I could be free, without encumbrances of guilt or passion or responsibility—the kind of burdens men take on eagerly and then don't know how to live with. I felt uncommitted and I was surprised to find the feeling pleasant.

It was after midnight when we reached Essie's home. "Would you like a cup of tea?" she offered.

"No etchings?"

"No etchings."

"Okay, I accept," I said cheerfully, and it was so much more pleasant than the aching unfulfillment that had dogged me for a lifetime whenever I was around Essie.

We had tea and toast and joked about our early years in London—laughter and no recriminations.

It was only when she reminded me of the kite I had made her, of warming our toes and our dinner on the makeshift fire, that our youthful joy in each other came back and made my heart heavy. For an instant, I saw her soft brown hair flying in the breeze as she raced across the lawns in Kensington Gardens, twenty-year-old Essie, my love. And now I saw her retreating into her memories as well. She dropped her head for a moment and that little lock of hair once again did its dance; it was the dance that had charmed me from the first moments we met. We were both full of emotion now. True to form Essie quickly recovered and introduced the names of old friends, taking us off to safer ground.

When I saw her surreptitiously look at her watch, I stood up.

"You're tired, Essie."

"I'm sorry, Max. It's just that I have to be up early again. I don't mean to be rude."

"It's fine," I assured her, and it really was. Something had been resolved; I couldn't define what, or how it had happened. I just knew I could leave her then without regrets. The whole nature of my unfulfilled longing for her had undergone a change. A line of half-remembered poetry flitted through my mind:

She walks in beauty like the night
Of cloudless climes and starry skies

I couldn't possess her any more than I could the stars, but I could always love her from a distance and feel fulfilled just in knowing that we shared the same universe and that she loved me, too.

I went back to England the next day. There didn't seem any point in staying in Jerusalem any longer. For once, Jeremy, Simon and Tiffany were all home and we sat for hours around the dining-room table, laughing and exchanging news. Ruth had made a wonderful dinner in honor of the rarity of everyone being in the same place at the same time. I had a "God's in his heaven, all's right with the world" feeling, and it seemed as though I hadn't felt that way for an eternity. The boys were doing well in their studies and seemed to be maturing, turning from sullen teenagers into surprisingly nice human beings. Tiffany was radiant, no doubt due to a romantic entanglement that for once was going well. All the strain of that ghastly period after Ruth's affair seemed to have dissipated as they listened with interest to some of my Lebanon stories. I knew the truth behind the old adage, "No man's a hero to his own valet," so it was doubly satisfying that—brief as it might be—at this particular moment, my family seemed to regard me with fondness and admiration.

When the kids had all disappeared after dinner to their various activities, Ruth and I had the house to ourselves. I hadn't finished unpacking, but it didn't seem important. I patted the sofa for Ruth to sit beside me, the sound of the dishwasher humming contentedly from the kitchen.

"Welcome home," she said softly.

"I wasn't away for so long."

"I didn't mean in Lebanon," she began diffidently.

"I know."

We didn't speak for a while, but the silence was companionable, not uncomfortable. I took her hand, and the light reflected from her gold wedding band.

"Ruth"—I cleared my throat—"there's something I didn't tell you."

She waited. I kept my eyes on the wedding ring, unsure how to proceed. "While I was in Lebanon, I ran into Essie. It was an amazing coincidence. And then I saw her again in Jerusalem." Because she didn't comment, I blundered on. "Nothing happened, nothing at all. We just went out to dinner and talked, and somehow, that was fine. It was all I wanted in the end."

"Essie rang me, after Lebanon," Ruth said quietly. "She just wanted to reassure me that you were fine; she didn't realize I didn't know you'd left, that you'd gone to Jerusalem."

I felt myself redden. "I wasn't trying to deceive you, I just thought you'd draw the wrong conclusions, think I was trying to pay you back or something."

"Were you?"

"No—not even subconsciously. That incident is behind us. I realize now how I contributed to it. But what's important is us, our family." She squeezed my hand, but didn't speak. I tried to find a way to verbalize my feelings. "Marriage is an emotion in itself, Ruth. I could give up every other feeling, but this— what we've built, and what we have—this is my safe harbor. Without this, I couldn't survive."

The kids came home, one by one, as we lay close to each other in the dark, her pretty hair—titian this month—tickling my chin. Each time a key grated in the lock and we heard the front door close, I felt close to completion. When finally all five of us were under the one roof, I knew an all-encompassing peace that seemed to have resolved my restlessness. I'd achieved something truly significant in my life, the happiness of my family.

The next morning I dashed into my study on the way to work to look for my briefcase. I halted just inside the door, the shock almost knocking me sideways. Just above my desk, Ruth had taken down the London fog painting and replaced it with her long-hidden portrait of Essie. There she was, immortalized forever at nineteen, Essie of the wild enthusiasms and joy in life. Now, of course, she was a woman of Jerusalem, mature as I was. In my mind's eye, I saw her against the backdrop of Jerusalem where she'd chosen to live her life.

I saw a city of stone, mellowed by the sun, in a land of iron. I saw its walls and citadels, turrets, domes, and minarets. I saw her there in changing seasons—pearly winter dawn, cloudless blue summer. I would not forget Jerusalem, just as I would not forget Essie. But she was a fond memory, gone like my youth, and no longer a threat. My wise Ruth realized it now, too.

I picked up my bag, and closed the door, and went on with my life.

THE END